dark future

GOLGOTHA RUN

AMERICA, TOMORROW. A world laced with paranoia, dominated by the entertainment industry and ruled by the corporations. A future where the ordinary man is an enslaved underclass and politics is just a branch of showbiz. Welcome to the Dark Future.

Eddie Kalish makes a terrible mistake when he stops to help a pretty nurse stranded in the desert. Before long, he's mixed up in a conspiracy involving experiments on human bodies. Plunged into all-out corporate war over a mysterious artefact, this country boy is going to have to use all his skills to come out alive.

dark future

GOLGOTHA
RUN

dave stone

A Black Flame Publication
www.blackflame.com

First published in Great Britain in 2005 by BL Publishing, Games Workshop Ltd., Willow Road, Nottingham NG7 2WS, UK.

Distributed in the US by Simon & Schuster, 1230 Avenue of the Americas, New York, NY 10020, USA.

10 9 8 7 6 5 4 3 2 1

Cover illustration by Jaime Jones.

ISBN 13: 978 184416 237 6
ISBN 10: 1 84416 237 0

A CIP record for this book is available from the British Library.

Printed in the UK by Bookmarque, Surrey, UK.

AMERICA, TOMORROW.

My fellow Americans —

I am speaking you today from the Oval Office, to bring you hope and cheer in these troubling times. The succession of catastrophes that have assailed our once-great nation continue to threaten us, but we are resolute.

The negative fertility zone that is the desolation of the mid-west divides east from west, but life is returning. The plucky pioneers of the new Church of Joseph are reclaiming Salt Lake City from the poisonous deserts just as their forefathers once did, and our prayers are with them. And New Orleans may be under eight feet of water, but they don't call it New Venice for nothing.

Here at the heart of government, we continue to work closely with the MegaCorps who made this country the economic miracle it is today, to bring prosperity and opportunity to all who will join us. All those unfortunate or unwilling citizens who exercise their democratic right to live how they will, no matter how far away from the comfort and security of the corporate cities, may once more

rest easy in their shacks knowing that the new swathes of Sanctioned Operatives work tirelessly to protect them from the biker gangs and NoGo hoodlums.

The succession of apparently inexplicable or occult manifestations and events we have recently witnessed have unnerved many of us, it is true. Even our own Government scientists are unable to account for much of what is happening. Our church leaders tell us they have the unknown entities which have infested the datanets in the guise of viruses at bay.

A concerned **citizen** asked me the other day whether I thought we were entering the Last Times, when Our Lord God will return to us and visit His Rapture upon us, or whether we were just being tested as He once tested his own son. My friends, I cannot answer that. But I am resolute that with God's help, we shall work, as ever, to create a glorious future in this most beautiful land.

Thank you, and God Bless America.

President Estevez

Brought to you in conjunction with the GenTech Corporation.

Serving America right.

[Script for proposed Presidential address, July 3rd 2021. Never transmitted.]

who is the real benedicta?

A BENEDICTA I knew, who filled the very world with the Ideal, whose eyes burned with the desire for majesty, beauty, glory and all that has us believe in the immortal.

But this miracle of a girl was just too beautiful to live; she died, therefore, but a few days after I met her – and it was I alone who buried her, on a day when Spring swung her censer even in the cemeteries themselves. It was I alone who buried her, potted in a coffin of a wood fragrant and imperishable as any chest of India.

And as my eyes were glued to the graveyard of my treasure, I saw quite suddenly a diminutive individual bearing a quite singular resemblance to the deceased, who, stamping on the fresh-dug ground with hysterical and somewhat bizarre violence, cried: "I'm the Benedicta! The real deal! And to punish you for your blindness, and your self-delusion, you shall love me as I am!"

"No!" I cried in fury. "No! No! No!" And in the rage of my refusal, I stamped upon the earth so violently that my leg sank to the knee into the fresh-dug grave. And like a wolf caught in a trap, there I remain – attached, perhaps for all time, to the grave in which my Ideal still rots.

All the same, though; I suppose a quick one wouldn't be entirely out of the question.

- with profound apologies to Charles Baudelaire

to the public

BEFORE GOING DOWN among you to pull out your decaying teeth, your running ears, your tongues full of sores,

Before breaking your putrid bones,

Before opening your cholera-infested belly and taking out as use for fertilizer your too-fatted liver, your ignoble spleen and your diabetic kidneys,

Before tearing out your ugly sexual organ, incontinent and slimy,

Before extinguishing your appetite for beauty, ecstasy, sugar, philosophy, mathematical and poetic metaphysical pepper and cucumbers,

Before disinfecting you with vitriol, cleansing you and shellacking you with passion,

Before all that,

We shall take a big antiseptic bath,

And we warn you,

We are murderers.

Manifesto signed by Ribemont-Dessiagnes and read by seven people at the Grand Palais des Champs Elysées, Paris, 5th February 1920

preLiminary
Information:
deathLess in
des moines

ARTIE NEWBEGIN WAS looking in the bathroom mirror, watching (at last count, the last time he had counted) four thousand, two hundred and thirty-nine fragments of face looking back at him.

Of course, that figure had long lost any kind of meaning by now; he had smacked a fist into the mirror any number of times since then (breaking three fingers the last time, which had actually been quite painful for a few seconds).

The mildew was out of control between the cracks again, Artie noted, congealing over any number of the smaller shards. The overall effect was a little like looking at the surface of a jewel-strewn swamp.

There was no real point in looking in the mirror in any case, nothing to do or worth doing with anything he might find in there, should the shattered visage ever suddenly cohere into something whole and complete.

That face, reassembled, would be a perfect thirty (the mature prime, the optimal point before the human metabolic flipover into catabolism) with no trace of toxin-contamination even to the point of a mild hangover.

The teeth pristine and cavity- and tartar-free, courtesy of the Bug, which knew the function of ostensibly inorganic compounds in the body, and knew, by and large, the differences between benign and malign bacteria. The beard would be a fixed, grown-out and somewhat straggly length, the Bug never having quite gotten its nonexistent head around the entirely human-level concept of shaving.

The hair on the head, interestingly enough, would be thick and lustrous and supremely manageable. Everyone had *fantastic* hair these days, which might or might not say something about whoever it was who had designed the Bug in the first place, before it had escaped. Almost certainly it had been a *he,* with a bad case of male-pattern baldness, for starters.

The bathroom was in an apartment, and the apartment was in a block, in what had once been downtown Des Moines, through which the wind whistled. Nothing much had changed, really, despite the pressure of the years inside Containment. Run-down, certainly, but still ticking over. Cars in the streets and the buses ran their routes a time out of three and most of them packed with those who still worked at some daily occupation or other.

The postures of normalcy must be maintained, Artie thought – rather in the same way that he himself would go to bed at night, when the Dome overhead polarised to black, and lie there sleepless.

And then, in the morning, going into the bathroom, even though there was nothing to do there, and going through the motions, before going out to make a killing.

THE WELCOME WAGON was sleek and black and looked like death on wheels. In the Last Days, in the days before the Rapture Bug, a vehicle of this nature – used for the same general purpose, for example, by some governmental agency – would have been covert rather than overt, customised to look like a battered old baker's van or something to blend into the scenery.

Now, the sight of these utterly distinctive black trucks shuttling merrily through the Des Moines streets warmed the

immortal hearts of people in their thousands. It was a bit like catching sight of a fire appliance would have been, in the days before the Bug hit. The Welcome Wagons were a constant reminder that someone, somewhere, cared.

The process-and-containment facilities took up most of the space in the back and the cab was somewhat cramped for three; proximity converting those colleagues one might quite like ordinarily, or at least find tolerable at a distance, into your worst nightmare.

Artie was currently crushed in the middle of the seat between Mico and Alex, and Mico was demonstrating his new trick for the fifteenth time: smashing his fingers against the jamb of the spill-hatch and twisting the resulting fractured mess into a halfway-recognisable set of male genitalia – as he remembered them – before they reset under the Bug.

In the hysteria immediately after the Rapture Bug had hit, after the Quarantine and Containment that would form the basis of the Dome had come slamming down, that sort of thing had become quite commonplace. In the higher-end of the art circles – so far as a city like Des Moines had had a high-level circle of art – there had been a brief vogue for the kind of body-modification that put the Theatre of Mutilation to shame… brief, of course, because the reset mechanisms of the Bug made such changes ultimately meaningless even in the terms of the avant garde. If the transformations don't stick, and nobody gains or loses the slightest thing because of them, then there's simply no point.

In general life, of course, the world had for a while become full of people hurling themselves off rooftops or under trucks, hitting each other with sledgehammers and axes purely for the hell of it. For several months it had been a bit like living in a *Road Runner* cartoon without the invention or the wit.

Those who were naturally inclined to jump in front of trucks in any case soon tired of the sheer futility of it, gradually followed by the rest of the Contained. Only complete retards like Mico found sufficient amusement in such things to even bother now.

Alex was driving with a kind of teeth-gritted concentration, fighting blind impulses that might have had her hurling the Wagon through traffic, careless of what it might hit... and the darker impulses that might have her aiming the thing directly at a wall in the vain hope that this time suicide might work.

Alex had once been, functionally, female, and now looked even more so in certain secondary aspects. Excessively, freakishly so in terms of the days before the Bug – though of course that was absolutely standard here and now.

It was just another of those not exactly *well* thought-out, blanket customisations to the genome, reinforcing the suggestion that the mythical designers of the Bug had been male. Artie had vaguely wondered, more than once, if the enthusiasm with which Alex treated her work might come from some form of sublimated impulse of revenge. It was far more likely, though, that after all this time Alex was merely working on the same basis as anybody else.

Logging up the hours on her Account. Working herself to death.

Now, Artie tried to ignore Mico's rather asinine antics by making a show of reading his clipboard, skimming through the client-list of those fortunate souls who had made enough on their Accounts to warrant the Welcome Wagon's current attention.

The process of monetary commerce was as good a way of keeping score as anything else – always provided that there was some mechanism for circumventing that process by pure luck.

One of the names on the list was marked with a cheerful little skull-and-crossbones. One of the *truly* lucky souls, picked completely at random from the general populace whether they had enough in their Account or not.

It had been months since Artie had been handed a genuine charity case – and he decided that it was just the thing to make him feel happier about the world, however temporary that happiness might be.

He'd been feeling so down lately. This might be just the thing he needed.

Artie Newbegin basked for a moment in the warm glow of anticipated altruism. Then he gave Alex the target and she punched up a location.

IT WAS LATER. Artie's shoulder was still quite painful – a kind of ghost-injury pain in the way that amputees had once had ghost limbs. It would fully take a half hour or so to clear up.

The procedure had started out well. They had parked the Welcome Wagon in a dedicated slot and deployed; located the precise position of the client in his apartment by way the ultrasonics, knocked a hole in the wall by way of clamp-mines and burst inside, Artie diving in low and doing it all totally by the book.

It had to be quick and sudden or you lost half of the point of it. Artie had smack-shackled the target's ankles to the floor, the electromagnetic concussion-bolts biting solidly into old, cured wood, and then gotten out of the way in a hurry so that Mico could shove the target over like the schoolyard bully that Mico once, presumably, at some point, had been. Mico's aptitude for this part of the procedure, and his general demeanour, strongly suggested this.

Mico and Alex held then the client – he was a *client* rather than a *target*, now – while while Artie used the buzzsaw, then hauled the upper body back, fighting against the phenomic homing-mechanisms that were even now, not to put too fine a point upon it, cutting in.

More smack-shackles on the arms and then back to the lower body to nailgun in the spikes and crampons that would secure it while they dealt with the tricky business of the head.

Using the buzzsaw, though, was always a risky business. It was quick but imprecise. Artie found that he had cut right through a vertebra, the smaller part of which chose that moment to detach and physically *shoot* for the larger part still attached to the pelvis… blasting through Artie's shoulder in the manner of the sort of pistol round that, in the old days, left people's arms hanging off.

And for just an instant, it had.

It had been a messy, complicated wound. It had taken almost a full minute for Artie's arm to reattach itself and for the gross physical damage to heal. The subtleties of trauma-healing had taken a few minutes more, and Artie's clumsiness had slowed them down in completing the first-stage vivisection.

It had not, to cut it short, been a clean kill. They had lost points on the timing. Credit-points they'd never see in their Accounts.

THEY WERE BACK in the Wagon again, the client safely packed away in the GenTech containment cells, heading for the depot, the multiple airlock access-hatches in the side of the Dome.

Sometimes, Artie thought, he could hear the head and hands and feet and jointed sections of arm rattling around and hammering inside the cells, but that of course was nonsense. A failure of containment to the point where even sound waves could escape would probably result in a fusion-cell blowout that would level buildings (though not of course, ultimately, the people in them) for half a mile around.

At the depot, by way of classified and carefully-controlled procedures, the various bodily components would be obliterated on the subatomic level and the lucky client at last given respite. An end to a life turned utterly meaningless and which, ordinarily, so far as humans reckon time, would have simply never stopped.

The procedures were extraordinarily expensive and complex, thus explaining the comparative rarity of their use, and why the likes of Artie, Alex, Mico – and for that matter every other living soul under the Des Moines Quarantine-and-Containment Dome – worked like dogs in the hope of one day being able to afford those procedures for themselves.

It had never occurred to them to wonder just what Gen-Tech itself got out of the arrangement – and even if it had, it was doubtful that they would have cared.

It didn't matter. Nothing mattered. They had seen the future and what the future held… and it held nothing but an endless, sleepless night of small, unwanted resurrections.

defauLt settings:
tooLing up

THE SEVERCY SISTERS hit them as they went through Checkpoint 9.

The gangcult had been stalking them for maybe ten miles, segueing in on one or other of the outriders to have an exploratory crack then peeling off, weighing up the defence-response. Now the core mass of them piled it on, coming in from both sides.

"The Sisters are small fry," Eddie Kalish said, quick-scanning the pattern-recognition specs and stats streaming across his Testostorossa's HUD. "They're just little girls with a grudge. No real kill power to speak. They don't care about the Brain Train – they're just coming in pincer-wise to knock off the front-runner."

"*Yeah, well,*" the Testostorossa said, diodes rippling on its voice-display, "*that would be us. What's the matter, faggot? Too much of a fag to wanna screw some girlies?*"

"I just think it's a waste." Inwardly some large part of Eddie groaned. He didn't mean any of this macho bullshit, but the Testostorossa was getting to him. He was starting to get the idea that killing people with an asinine quip on your lips was just flat-out murder.

Through the shotgun window a girl in torn leather and spikes leant from her quad-bike and swung what appeared to be an exact copy of a medieval morningstar. It looked pretty lethal, but the business end of it rebounded from the monatomic carbon shell of the Testostorossa to no effect what-soever.

The Sister snarled in pique. She couldn't have been more than sixteen years old.

"Anyhow," Eddie said. "The kids just aren't tooled-up enough to hurt us."

"Yeah, but they're drawing attention to us," the Testostorossa said. *"Lots of other fuckers out there, waiting to sit up and take notice – and they're packing enough heavy stuff to make us go bang-splat."*

Seemingly of their own accord, multidirectional scatterguns extended, locked and loaded.

"I'm scraping these bitches off us as of now," the Testostorossa said. *"You just keep that pinhead of yours on driving me."*

Eddie gunned the turbo-acceleration and sighed. How the hell had he ever gotten himself into this?

first quadrant
Las vitas fault

FROM THE DOORWAY a roscoe said "Kachow!" and a slug
creased the side of my noggin. Neon lights exploded
inside my think-tank... She was as dead as a stuffed
mongoose... I wasn't badly hurt. But I don't like to be
shot at. I don't like dames to be rubbed out when I'm
flinging woo at them.

"Killer's Harvest"
Spicy Detective
July 1938

radio none

"THIS IS WWAXZY News, every hour, on the hour – sponsored by Big Easy Gumbo, steaming bowls of fishy goodness just like your big fat Momma used to make. Big Easy Gumbo is a property-division of Eidolon Industries SA. Big Easy Gumbo and Your Big Fat Momma are registered trademarks. All rights reserved.

"And our top story, of course, are the rumours that chart-topping B-girl Freak-E has split with her longtime manager and boyfriend, Slee-Z. Freak-E, who is currently topping every corporate datanet download chart with her international superhit 'Be My Pimp', is said to be distraught and was unavailable for comment. Slee-Z, on the other hand, couldn't say enough to our waiting reporters. 'Yo, b____h, where's my f__king money, ho? Think I'm gonna make you a star and then let you start s__king the next n___a's d__k, think again, b___h. Watch yo back yo.'

"Latest reports suggest that Freak-E is currently in talks with king of the New York hip-hop scene, Big Master X, about representing her. You can bet we'll be bringing you more news on this one as is happens, folks.

"Other news: across the pond in Merrie Olde England, the Leader of His Majesty's Loyal Opposition has criticised PM Peter Mandelson's support for the US carpet-bombing of the Confederated Republics of the Congo as, quote, 'The act of a simpering and cowardly little freak, so far up the US President's crack you'd need a pickaxe to get him out, and the world would be a cleaner place if he'd ran down his mother's leg.'

"The President was unavailable for comment. The PM himself is currently out of reach of our reporters. The Grand Old man of British politics, however, Sir John Lennon, has issued the statement that, 'This outburst is simply not how we did politics in my day, and it shames me deeply that this man might be seen, by way of party membership, to have any connection with me in the slightest. I wish to disassociate myself from this execrable little s__t and his statements entirely.'

"You go tell 'em, Johnny! Rock the House.

"Closer to home, the mysterious outbreak of mass hallucination down in Los Bolivaros has now been explained by declassified footage showing seconded DEA agents burning genetically-modified coca fields as part of a joint operation with *Securidad Internaçionale*. The hallucinogenic effects of the toxins released, from a crop destined to become a major component in a whole new breed of Designer Crack, convinced befuddled locals that the very gaping Maw of Hell had opened up to spew creatures born of neither man nor woman, spawn of the Ever and Eternal Screaming Night.

"Uncontrolled bleeding from the eyes and ears of these locals was purely psychosomatic – to believe that creatures spawning from the ever and eternal screaming night truly existed, in any way, shape of form, would be just plain *loco*.

"'Besides,' sez Drugs Czar Karenna Gore Schiff, 'anyone around to actually witness these hallucinations was drug-running scum, and shooting them in the head to put them out of their misery was better than they deserved.'

"That's the main news on this hour. Now here's Freak-E with 'Be My Pimp'…"

1.

Eddie Kalish crawled on his belly and squinted through the good lens of his goggles. He'd picked them up maybe a year ago, from the crushed remains of a lone motorsickle package-runner who hadn't needed them anymore.

The mutated coyote that had killed the runner hadn't wanted them either, leaving them on the corpse after it had fed.

Coyote didn't have the smarts, or the manipulation, to deal with truly human technology. They just set up these crude and dumb but incredibly complicated apparatuses for dropping rocks on people, without ever quite understanding why.

The bad lens of the goggles was crazed and crusted with liquid-crystal chemicals leaking from the multiple lead-glass sandwich. The good lens, though, could still track and target, zoom in on images and enhance them with some degree of clarity.

Eddie zoomed in, somewhat ineptly, down the *mesa* to the plain beyond, where steel and polypropylene and meat were being systematically taken apart.

* * *

THE BIG BEHEMOTH tankers of a GenTech Corp road-train had fallen foul of a jackgang — a variety of gangcult that, through a tortuous network of fronts and double-blinds, had a connection to some actual Incorporate patron. The patron supplied funding and a market for loot. This meant that large-scale hijacking was practicable, as opposed to pulling down the smalltime shit for the pure hell of it.

The jackgang had actively planned this, maybe over months. Whoever might be funding them had seriously tooled them up.

The road-train front runner, in his zippy little Toledo, had run straight over undetectable carbon fibre tyre-slashers, and smack into crash-barriers that sprang up under one-shot servos. The outriders were taken out by shoulder-mounted STS projectiles, closing off the turning-circle, and the mobile Command and Control unit by mortar, effectively boxing the road-train in.

The jackgangers had then moved in for the kill... only to find that they had walked into a trap of their own. With the concussion of detonation-bolts, three of the Behemoths had split open along pre-stressed fracture lines to reveal GenTech shock-troops armed with heavy-duty weaponry of their own.

In the world of physics, equally matched forces tend towards an equilibrium. In the world of humans possessed of heavy-duty armament, equally matched forces result in sheer bloody chaos.

Eddie decided to leave them to it. Only when the last bodies — or their component parts — were still, did he climb to his feet and head for the battered little Kraut Karrier RV that counted for everything he owned in the world, and thence down the dirt track leading down from the *mesa* to the plain.

A MISDIRECTED MORTAR shell had totalled the hauling rig — even if a jackganger or a trooper had survived in a state to drive it, the road-train wasn't going anywhere soon.

One of the refrigerated Behemoths, one of those that had been carrying the payload rather than troopers, was breached

and spilling packaged human organs. Many of the packages were split and already spoiling in the New Mexico heat. The smell was already attracting scouts from the feral dog packs that roamed the wasteland.

Eddie hefted an automatic rifle and sighted on one of the canine scouts, preparing to empty whatever was in the clip into it, but the dog caught his attention on it and backed off sullenly. Things would be different when the pack arrived, but for the moment a single dog was no match for an armed human.

Eddie was relieved. He was unsure how to operate the somewhat overcomplicated control mechanisms of the rifle anyway. Besides, the gun was still chained to the surprisingly heavy mass of a severed forearm, and he didn't feel up to trying to detach it.

He dropped the arm and gun to the blood-washed dirt and looked down on their previous owner. The guy was mangled and paralysed but still just barely alive. One of the jackgangers.

Eddie had always been confused by the way in which some people could take a look at some gangcult, read the crawling mass of insignia and tattoos and go, "Aha! These are obviously the Clan of the Leaping Viper, operating out of the Los Palamos barrios and the scourge of the area between InterStat checkpoints 703 and 709 inclusive!" and the like.

He strongly suspected, since the only way you could walk away from a gangcult was to leave them dead, you could say what you like about them after you did – and so these people who had walked away just made all the tough-sounding names up.

It gave you more kudos to say, "Just took out the dreaded Tungsten Razorbacks," than, "Jeb and Earl Terwilliger and a bunch of their good ole pals tried to jump us with shotguns, but we had a Gatling so we like just as to totally slaughtered them," that was for sure.

All Eddie Kalish could see, looking down at the jackganger, was a big and mean-looking sack of crap who would have been able to tear him, Eddie Kalish, a new hole and use it as an ashtray had he been in any way mobile.

"Scavenger rat-fuck-bastard piece of scum!" the jackganger croaked as Eddie went through the remains of his clothes looking for anything he might use. "Don't do nothin' save as to slime in there and rob the dead."

"Yeah, well." Eddie examined the sharp and well-kept hunting knife he had unearthed. "It's a living."

LEAVING THE JACKGANGER to his own devices, Eddie was feeling pretty good about himself – just like he had refrained from slitting the jackganger's throat out of profound moral sentiment rather than simply not having the guts.

Closer to the centre of the smoking carnage, the bodies were far less intact and just as dead as it was possible to get.

A fortune in weaponry, both on the troopers and the jackgangers, looked to be more-or-less undamaged, but Eddie paid it no heed. A hunting knife was okay, that was useful – but you carried any more than that and there was no way anyone you might run into would let you live, crawl and beg for your life as you might.

Eddie was looking for food and medical supplies – commodities he could use, and sell to those few people he knew who were of a kind to be grateful. Grateful enough to barter, anyhow, if not pay actual credit. There was a girl over in Las Vitas, for sure, who would reciprocate a dose of fast-acting, one-shot antibiologics in the manner that had her needing the dose in the first place–

Something wrong.

Scavenging rat-bastard Eddie might have been, but you didn't survive the nearly seventeen years he had by going against those ratlike instincts.

He stayed there immobile, semi-crouched, ears alive and alert to the sound that had sounded wrong amongst the creaking of ruptured Behemoth skins, the crackle of flames and the distant howls of feral dogs.

There it came again. A faint and tenebrous clanking. Not the inadvertent sounds of someone still, somehow, alive and strong enough to be coming for you. More the sounds

of someone trying, weakly and against all hope, to attract help.

It was coming from one of the Behemoths other than those that had contained troops. A slew of genetically-engineered offal, however, was not falling from the blown hatch.

Cautiously, reflexes wound up tight to flinch away from any sign of danger, Eddie moved in closer.

Even Eddie himself would have been hard-pressed to express what he had expected to find, other than the satisfaction of simple rat-like curiosity that it for the moment cost him nothing to satisfy. Maybe there was some incredibly special and valuable cargo in there, the nature of which he could not so much as begin to guess.

As it turned out, the nature of the cargo surpassed his barely-formed imaginings.

The inside of the tanker looked like a cross between a palace and a med-centre – though for all Eddie knew, this was what the rooms of rich people always looked like when they went into hospital. Archaic-looking brass fixtures and silken hangings and a big four-poster bed.

On the bed, plugged into bloodpacks and bleeping med-units, the withered and unconscious figure of an old man. There was something about his form that seemed unsettlingly odd and wrong: that strange, coma-case distinctness that comes from remaining utterly immobile while still being alive.

Eddie didn't particularly notice, far less care. His eyes were riveted on the girl who sat, or rather slumped, beside the bed.

She was in… you really had to call it a *costume*, rather than clothing or a uniform. A nurse's costume, the already short dress hiked up an inch or so to expose the black silk of her panties, garters to black stockings and spiked heels. One of the stockings had a ladder in it.

The costume tried but spectacularly failed to contain breasts which seemed to have a gravitational pull of their own – they certainly had a pull on the eyes of one Eddie Kalish. Nipples the size of small grapes strained against the thin fabric as if desperate to burst through. The ensemble was topped off by a

perky little cap perched on platinum-blonde cascades of hair, and cosmetics applied to overstatedly libidinous effect. The bright red lipstick, for example, was applied in the manner suggesting that the wearer had left a large portion of it on whatever she had just finished sucking.

The end result was, in effect, something to make that portion of the human race with a Y-chromosome howl like one of the approaching dogs outside and fall instantly in love. At least, for a time. Or as many times as might be allowed.

All in all, it was something of a pity that she had been gutshot. Shrapnel from the stray round that had breached the Behemoth hatch. Things slid around in the hole.

For all this, against all physical human possibility, she was still alive.

"Please…" she rasped to Eddie as he looked on horrified and wide-eyed. "Get us out… get us to GenTech. As much money as you want… more money than you can imagine… just get us to GenTech…"

2.

HALFWAY TO LAS VITAS a shitstorm hit them like a hammer – literally, in this case. Amongst the miscellaneous crap that fell from the sky along with the hail, and which gave these storms their name, was a collection of crudely-moulded tools of the sort used in the New Soviet dreadnought yards, clear across the world.

Inferior lug-wrenches rattled on the RV's roof, and what might once have been a seven-pound sledgehammer punched a neat hole in the windshield, size of a soup plate, to land in the shotgun seat as an amorphous, smoking lump.

"Jeezus!" Eddie beat at the incipient fire through the reek of scorching vinyl and stuffing, blistering his hands. It only occurred to him later that he could have simply popped the shotgun door and kicked the smoking lump of low-grade steel out.

Then again, exposing the interior of the RV to the storm directly would as like to have had him shredded on the spot.

As suddenly as it had started, the storm stopped, as if a switch had been thrown.

Even in a terrain of desert heat punctuated by violent squalls and flash-floods, weather shouldn't happen this fast.

Something inside insisted, blindly, that the sheer speed of the transitions was wrong.

LITTLE DEKE – AND you'd better believe that no one made jokes about his name to his face – had explained all this to Eddie once.

They had been grabbing a couple of cool ones after junking the almost complete wreck of a Malaysian caterpillar-treaded logging rig deposited up on the *mesa* by a particularly violent storm. This was back in the days when things had been cool between Eddie and Deke, and Eddie was working for food and a place to sleep behind electrowire.

Eddie had advanced the proposition that the shitstorms were maybe being done to the world by aliens – to the vague extent of what he imagined aliens to be. It seemed to be about as strange and pointless as corn-holing rednecks out of their pickup trucks and messing around with cows, that was for sure.

"What the *fuck* would aliens be doing, going around dropping shit on folk?" Little Deke had told him. "They got all those there laser cannon and tactical nukes and shit. Or they would have if they even existed in the first place. But they don't. Not like you mean. They proved it. There's nothing out there in space we can use. It's empty. That's what space *means*."

Little Deke was the richest man Eddie knew, and he knew things. One of his first acts, on settling down in his junker's yard outside of Las Vitas, had been to install an array of parabolic dishes, hooking him into the global datanet, TV-syndication and all manner of other shit. Eddie had been forced to bow, outwardly at least, to his wisdom.

"So where does it come from?" he'd asked Little Deke. "I mean, what causes it?"

"Skyhooks." Little Deke had gestured in a direction that to Eddie, who had less sense of compass-direction than of how you were supposed to tell one gangcult from another, could have been anywhere.

"Shit they're building out in Florida," Little Deke explained, "up there in Boston, whole bunch of other places. Run a

monomolecular wire down from a satellite and you can run shit up and down it like a fuckin' elevator."

"If there's nothing up there in space," mused Eddie, who thought he had spotted a logical flaw, "then why do the guys need an elevator to go up there?"

"Fuck should I know? Maybe all them rich corporate folks from the compound blocks like the view."

Deke took another pull on his Corona, noticed it was empty, scowled and flung it at a ferroconcrete stanchion, where it shattered. Most of the shards fell in a sawn-off oil drum that half-heartedly served as a recycling bin.

"All I know is, they seriously fuck up the weather," he said. "'A step-system of microclimatic tiers existing on the point of localised catastrophic cascade-collapse' or some such happy crap from Discovery Weather Channel. All I got from that was that the weather round these parts is frankly screwed. These days anything can fall out of the fuckin' sky."

MICROCLIMATIC TIERS ON the point of catastrophic cascade-collapse or not, Eddie still found it hard to imagine what kind of storm could pick up a bunch of tools and the suchlike from Smolensk, or wherever, transport it halfway around the globe then and dump it on some out of the way spot in New Mexico.

Or how it could be caused by someone just hanging what was basically a string from a satellite down in Florida. He just couldn't imagine the through-line of how it could be possible.

The point about that, though, was that when it actually happened, imagination was not required.

It was like the way that if the Lord God Almighty were to suddenly turn up, spraying lightning from his fingers and demanding sacrifice, you wouldn't start debating your belief in him or otherwise; you'd be casting around like a bastard and wondering where you could find the nearest fatted calf.

The engineered algae that permeated the blacktop of the main highways, and kept them in a state of constant self-repair,

was doing its stuff. Holes punched in the surface by hail and debris were knitting themselves together, the debris itself sinking as though dropped into a pool of engine oil.

Eddie could never quite work out how the algae knew the difference between garbage and, for example, a battered old Kraut Karrier piece of crap that was barely one step away from being garbage at the best of times. He worried about that, sometimes. He had visions of the blacktop yawning open one of these days and swallowing him up.

In any event, it was fortunate that Eddie had decided to risk the highway, as opposed to sticking to the dirt roads. A shit-storm out there would have churned the ground to mud, leaving him bogged down and stranded – whether for hours or days, it didn't matter in the present circumstance.

Even minutes might be too long.

Eddie turned the engine over and swung a glance back into the RV, which was more than somewhat cramped. The old guy was lying on the sprung fold-down bunk that had served as Eddie's bed these last few years, coma-still body loosely wrapped in mirror-reflective polymer sheeting like a pot roast in a microwave.

Tubes and wires ran from under the sheeting to modular portable medpacks, their inner workings pumping and whirring away with a sound like the insides of a notebook computer. Their displays were shut down to eke out the power remaining in their cells.

Eddie had lugged the old guy into the van and installed the med-packages under the semi-lucid instruction of the girl in the nurse's costume.

On first seeing her, he had assumed she was just that – a hooker in costume, hired by some rich old guy to go with the clinical technology that actually did the job.

She had known her business, though, even while going about the business of dying from the wound in her gut. Eddie had wondered if she couldn't have used some of the old guy's medical crap on herself, but she had insisted, quite vehemently, that there would be no point. The important thing was to get her charge to GenTech.

Her name, so Eddie gathered when she was lucid, was Trix Desoto.

Now Trix Desoto lay, curled up foetally and clutching her belly, on a couple of garbage sacks containing the old clothes that were pretty much all Eddie owned. Still alive, but in a bad way.

The sense of sheer *sex* she exuded, in collision with the bloody horror of her wound, made Eddie feel weird. It was like patching into a descrambled movie channel and suddenly realising you were watching pay-per-view snuff.

The wound beneath her interlaced fingers had stopped bleeding. Eddie knew enough, having seen enough people die even in his few tender years, to know this meant one of two things: blood-loss, shock and coma – or, if there was enough blood left for the heart to pump, lingering on for hours and days before the infection from her messed-up insides finally took her down.

She seemed to be going the second route. Burning and shaking with fever – and this seemed a little odd. It had just come on too *fast*, like the way that shitstorms came and went too fast to be possible, like a switch being thrown.

It was just in his mind, but he felt like he could feel the heat she was putting out, pulsing over his face like the radiation from a thermal element.

"Storm's over," Eddie told her. "We're moving again. Listen, you're not looking so good…"

"*Talekli lamo da ti saso ma, hasi de los padremaso tik de lama…*" The girl was babbling with delirium. "*Masa tu so gladji beri rama…*"

Somebody had once told Eddie that English was his second language, and he didn't have a first one. Even he could tell, though, that this wasn't any kind of language you could find on Planet Earth. It was like that Speaking in Tongues shit they did over at the Dog Soup Tabernacle up in Silver City.

"*… saso ti da mati namo, zara ti raguesta di la ramo…*"

"Listen," Eddie said. "What happens if you die? You die, what do I do? How do I get on this more money than I can imagine you were talking about?"

"... *maso si nami lama* – what the *fuck* are you talking about, you scavenging little shit?"

Instantly, Trix Desoto was lucid, and lifting her head to glare at him cold-eyed. It wasn't even like she was fighting off the pain. That switch thing yet again; a completely different person had been switched on in her like a light.

Eddie found himself feeling shamefaced under her direct and contemptuous gaze.

"All I mean is," he said, not a little shamefacedly, "is that I don't know what any of this is about. I don't know who to call. You die on me out here, how am I gonna know who to call?"

"Then my advice to you would be to drive like a mother-fucker and just hope I don't."

The light of coherence snapped off and her head fell back.

"Slami makto, shaba tlek na doura rashamateran..."

Eddie drove.

3.

Las Vitas was little more than a glorified truck stop: a settle-down because, what the hell, folks just sometimes still have to stop somewhere. A cluster of second-string services around the dead remains of a TexMexxon station.

The station itself had croaked near around twenty years ago, so far as those who were in a position to know had told Eddie Kalish. Bolt-on hydrogen-fusion technology had not been kind to the dealers from the days when vehicles needed their regular fix of hydrocarbons.

What Las Vitas had was communications. With the C&C rig totalled back at the site of the ambush, Las Vitas was the near-est place that Trix Desoto could make whatever calls she needed to make.

That, at least, had been the plan.

"Shit…" Eddie checked the scene and then just kept on going. "Gangcult hit it hard and serious – maybe the same guys did you. This was heavy-duty."

The big, vestigial *TexMexx* sign which had served as an accretion point for Las Vitas was down, the dishes strapped to its superstructure shattered or scattered. That had probably

been the first order of business: take out the comms before
they could get off a signal to the US Cav.

And vehicles that might have been stopping over were long
gone, save for a flipped-over garbage truck with a hole
punched through it. Prefab cabins were just smoking polycarbon shells; the jerry-built structures that had been thrown up
from local materials in the first place merely ash.

Reddish-brown smears dotted on the levelled concrete
expanse where trucks and road-trains had once parked; weird
little organic lumps that you didn't want to look at in case you
worked out what they were.

The ruins of Las Vitas still smoked gently. The fires had had
maybe an hour to burn down. If survivors were going to be
crawling out of – or back to – the wreckage then they would
have done it by now. Las Vitas had been zombie-towned – in
coming weeks and months it would turn into a ghost town,
but for the moment the meat was just too fresh.

Eddie kept his eyes on the pristine blacktop and just drove,
mind working furiously. Such as it was. Only one immediate
possibility occurred.

"Las Vitas is a bust," he said, wondering if Trix Desoto could
even hear him through her babbling. "There's only one thing
for it. We're gonna have to try Little Deke."

LAST TIME EDDIE Kalish had seen Little Deke had been in the
rear-view mirror, as the guy was bringing up a scattergun and
loosing off as Eddie tooled the stolen RV out of his compound.

Eddie had come across the thing, half-buried under a collection of old dune-buggy frames, and had wondered what it
was. He'd had the idea that Recreational Vehicles were supposed to be these big old sixteen-wheelers with a load the size
of a prefab house and dirt bikes slung across the back.

This was just a clunky little capsule barely bigger than any
street car.

Small enough that Eddie could imagine taking it and driving it away.

"It's a *Veedubya*," Little Deke had told him, spitting out the word along with a wet gob of thoroughly masticated *loco* weed. "Fuckin' Kraut Karrier. It's older than I am. Now get your sorry ass over here and help me strip down this piece of shit coolant system."

Eddie's thoughts had kept coming back to the little RV. He'd been working for Little Deke pretty much as long as he could remember – long enough that he didn't remember if Deke was any kind of family or just some guy.

Little Deke hadn't treated him particularly badly, but as he'd gotten older Eddie had realised that all he was, and what he was, was stuck there in the junkyard going nowhere.

There had just been nothing to keep him there. Eddie had taken to sleeping in the little RV, spent odd hours fixing it up, waited for his chance to swipe a working hydrogen cell, and then just got the hell out. There was a big, wide world out there, apparently, and Eddie had wanted a taste of it.

In the end, he had never got so far. A couple of years aimless wandering, never pulling down the kind of score that might get him further… and now he was crawling back.

"Cut him in on the money, he'll be fine," Eddie told Trix Desoto, not sure at this point whether she could hear and understand him or not. "That is, if he doesn't just shoot me on sight."

THE ELECTROWIRE STOOD dark and silent – which meant nothing, on account of the fact that several million volts running through steel mesh gives no visible sign.

The gate was held securely shut by a heavy-gauge electromag-lock, and there was no sign of movement behind it save for the vague flapping of polymer sheeting and the like amongst the junk.

A camera tracked back and forth in its housing to regard them, a light blinking on its faceplate under the lens.

After a while the lock buzzed and low-yield servos cut in to swing the gate-sections open, outward, against the force of gravity that held them customarily shut.

"Well, he hasn't shot us yet," said Eddie. "That might be a sign."

Eddie nosed the van into the compound, alert for the first flash of movement.

No sight or sound of threat at all... not even from the skunk/rottweiler hybrids that, he now recalled, Little Deke left the run of the compound to when not around.

Dogs with skunk glands grafted into them, together with microelectronic triggering implants. Kind of like those money-packages that spray you when you try to rip them off – although money-packages didn't have the kind of jaws that could tear you a new one before they went off.

Back in the day, the creatures had been trained to recognise Eddie's scent and not attack; these days, Eddie wasn't so sure, even if they were old enough to remember him being around.

Ah, well. The lack of skunkdogs meant that Little Deke was going to be around, somewhere. Eddie supposed that he could be holed up somewhere in the piles of junk, waiting and drawing a sniper-bead on him, but he knew that wasn't Little Deke's style.

If he was still angry, after a couple of years, he wouldn't be exactly subtle: he'd just come at them roaring and blazing away.

Eddie shut off his engine. Off to one side he could hear the hum of the meth-generators that supplied the compound and its fence with power, but the old AmTrak boxcar which served Little Deke as a domicile was dark and silent.

No lights burning even though it was getting on for dusk. The big floods lashed to various items in the junk piles and lit the yard for night work stood dark and dormant.

Eddie left the van and made his cautious way to the AmTrak car. "Deke? You there? I just wanna say that..."

SNAPSHOTS.

Eddie would never have a clear and sequential memory of the adrenalin of panic kicking in. Just telegraphic snapshots of single, discrete images, like the output of the random camera of the eye jump-cut together:

The extensive collection of antique porno (genuine paper magazines) which Little Deke had preferred to the girls available in Las Vitas — mylar bags ruptured and their contents shredded by automatic fire.

The telecommunications unit that plugged into the signals from the parabolic dishes outside, smashed to pieces by some blunt implement. Maybe the butt of an automatic rifle.

The breadboarded-together collection of personal computer circuitry that served as a maintenance-and-control deck for the compound's security devices — like the cameras and the lock on the gate that had so recently let Eddie inside. The monitor screens had been punched in, but the deck had been left relatively intact. Someone had placed what looked like a big, black polypropylene-skinned slug on the keyboard. It rippled, operating the keys, and thus the compound-security, under remote control.

The headless body of Little Deke, the 450-pound bulk of it hanging from the articulated gimbal-harness he used to get around indoors. There was surprisingly little blood; the neck had either been cauterised by whatever had decapitated him, or Little Deke's heart just hadn't been up to producing a gusher from his sheer mass.

In any case, Eddie didn't think about all this until later. At the time all he saw were the snapshots, the flash-flash-flash like you get in movies that tell you what the basic story is — and the story was, at this point, that one Eddie Kalish was now in the total shit and it was time to get out.

Forget about learning the details or any happy shit like that; just get the *fuck* out.

Eddie jackrabbited from the AmTrak and flung himself towards the van — just as big Kliegs clashed on, slamming the world into a monochromatic state of dead black and magnesium white. They weren't the junkyard floods; they were coming from outside.

In the shock and dazzle, before his eyes were overwhelmed, Eddie caught sight of the shapes behind the chain-link and

lights. Blocky trucks – not the lashed–together bikes and pods of a jackgang. They were military spec.

"GRAB YA ANKLES, SWEETHEART!" an amplified voice barked, out beyond the wire. And the thump-thump-thump of an annoying and generic Boystown Disco Beat started up. Regulation issue psycho-warfare protocol.

"JUST YOU RELAX AND TAKE IT EAAASY!" the amplified voice came over the mix. "NEOGEN GONNA TAKE YA, JUST RELAX AND TAKE IT EASY!"

Detonation cutters sliced the fence on two sides. Through the flare and dazzle Eddie saw the dark figures hazing in.

4.

UP ON THE mesa, *out past the burning remains of Las Vitas, a pollutant-mutated scorpion was in the process of laying its eggs in the still barely-living flesh of a hairless dog.*

There was no one to see this, and therefore no one to remark on how the air around scorpion and dog now shimmered, how a sickly light hazed from their forms.

Instantly, as though some switch of unlife had been thrown, both arachnid and canine flesh crumbled into their component molecular parts, leaving nothing but skeletal remains and a perfectly intact chitionous husk.

"WE GOT TROUBLES," Eddie said, slamming back into the van. "Looks like soldiers."

"TWO MINUTES TO SURRENDER," the bullhorn-voice boomed cheerfully, "THEN WE GET LETHAL. IT'S LIKE TOTALLY YOUR DECISION, GUY."

"Mercenaries," Trix Desoto said. "Delta-trained. NeoGen runs a cadre of them for hunting parties."

Eddie strained his eyes on the dead black shadows outside, imagining the stealthy figures as they silently and invisibly

took up position. He didn't actually hear and see anything, of course, on account of the meaning of the words "silent" and "invisible".

He wouldn't hear or see a thing, he realised with a cold sick certainty, until they dropped the hammer.

"MINUTE AND A HALF…" the bullhorn boomed. "SAY, YOU A SPIC, BOY? YOU A CATHERLICK? TIME FOR A COUPLE OF HAIL MARYS IF YOU *REALLY* FEEL THE NEED FOR A QUICK RATTLE ON THE ROSARIES!"

"Where the fuck did *that* come from?" Eddie muttered to himself. There might or might not have been some Hispanic in his parentage – it was about as likely as anything else – but he couldn't see what that had to do with anything.

"Destabilisation tactics," Trix Desoto said. "Like the disco. Keeping us off-balance for when they come in to take the package."

"Package?" Eddie said.

Trix Desoto indicated the supine form of the unconscious man.

"THAT'S THE BUNNY!" came the bullhorn. "NICE OF YOU TO GIVE US A GOOD LOOK AT THE MER-CHANDISE!"

For a second, Eddie was unaware of what the bullhorn guy had meant. He sat there in a cold sweat, looking at the van's interior light, trying to work it out.

Then he lurched towards it with a curse and shut the light off.

"CLEVER GUY!" came the bullhorn. "WE GOT NIGHT SIGHTS AND THERMAL-IMAGING SYSTEMS OUT THE ASS, MAN! YOU JUST LEFT YOURSELF BLIND AND IN THE DARK. THIRTY SECONDS!"

If there was one thing, absolutely one thing, that Eddie Kalish was not going to do it was turn the light back on again.

Besides, what with the spill-in from the big Kliegs outside, it didn't make any real difference. The guy was just trying to find another way to rattle him and keep him from doing something all resourceful and heroic.

Not that *that* made any difference, either. If the resourceful hero in Eddie Kalish was waiting to make itself known, it was taking its own sweet time about it.

"That's it, then," Eddie said. The choices had come down to sitting here and dying, or even pretending to believe in this "surrender" crap and dying in the open. "There's nothing we can do."

"Oh there's something we can do," said Trix Desoto. "There's something I can do."

Looking at her in the in the glare of the Kliegs, it finally percolated through Eddie what had been odd about her since he had made it back to the van. Gone was the delirious swinging between lucidity and alien-sounding gibberish.

Now she seemed entirely and unnaturally sanguine – and not in any sense relating to the catastrophic blood-loss from the wound in her gut.

In fact, she was looking pale but strangely healthy. The body in the comedy-nurse uniform seemed somehow bulkier and stronger.

It might have simply been the light, but Eddie thought he could see weird muscle-masses moving under the skin. Half-thoughts of vampires, of zombies, flashed through Eddie's mind. Walking corpses, monstrous after death.

"There's something I can do," Trix Desoto repeated, eyes a kind of burning black behind the slatted zebra-striping of light and shadow from the Kliegs. "And I'm going to do it now."

IN THE BURNING *ruins of Las Vitas, the flesh of any number of scavenging animals hazed instantly into molecular dust – along with the remaining flesh of that on which they were feeding.*

Is was not as if something were sucking some actual life-force, if that word can be made to mean anything in the first place. It was more as if something were feeding on some product of life-coherence…

COMMANDER THOMAS MARLON Drexler, heading up the wet-squad out of NeoGen, was suffering from a small gap in basic expectations.

The fact was that, over the years, military-grade command technology had evolved to the point where with a single and suitably controlled squad of operatives one could subvert the infrastructure and take command of an entire city or country.

Schematic analysis of anything from the power and informational grids to the plumbing, plus detailed psychologistical profiling of the principle characters amongst the enemy, ensured that force could be applied to critical targets with a zero-tolerance of error: the equivalent of assassinating Franz Ferdinand because you *really* hate a bunch of limpid individuals banging on about the corner of some forgotten field, and want to see the lot of them end up dead.

Such seriously shit-hot Control and Command equipment didn't come cheap, of course, but NeoGen supplied its Retrieval people with the best – especially if said people were going up against such an equally-matched rival as GenTech.

Such tactical control-processes had worked perfectly in the matter of setting some local jackgang on a GenTech road-train, manipulating the various factors in such a matter that the forces neutralized each other. Then Drexler and his squad had moved in to pick up the pieces... and hit that gap in expectations.

There was another factor on the board. And that factor, simply, was just some guy that nobody gave a flying fuck about.

There was not a single person who particularly knew or cared if he lived and died – and that was the problem right there. It was like some idiotic squit of a kid going up against a Grand Master in chess; the kid does things so flatly idiotic that it leaves the Grand Master momentarily flummoxed.

The kid and the package, together with the package's medical support, had fled the site of the road-train ambush just before Drexler and his NeoGen forces had arrived. Tracksat systems had pinpointed the little RV almost instantly, but the forces on the ground found themselves with a problem. NeoGen had come armed and ready to deal with GenTech or jackganger survivors; they were perfectly capable of leaving some escaping piece-of-crap van a smoking hole in the road

that not even micro-engineered algaeic heal-sealant would be able to fill.

What they did not have, however, was the capacity to intercept and stop it without damaging the package irreparably.

Tracksat extrapolation had showed that the van was heading for Las Vitas, and military-spec four-wheel drive had made it in half the time, even over rough terrain. Drexler had looked around the shithole and not reckoned much to it. Too many holes and corners. Street-fighting could get messy.

So Drexler and his boys had broken out their heavy-duty armament and removed the town from the equation.

He didn't feel particularly good about that, but then again he didn't feel bad either. It was just what you had to do, sometimes.

The only other place, within practical distance and with communications, had been the junker's yard here. Strategic modelling of all available factors placed the probability of containing the target here in the upper ninetieth percentile.

That, at least, was what MIRA had assured Commander Drexler. Drexler, on the other hand, was rapidly coming to the conclusion that MIRA was at this point just making it up off the top of her cybernetic head and winging it.

"What was that shit about calling the guy a spic?" he asked MIRA. "Plus all that, you know, religious stuff?"

Ordinarily, the Mobile Intrusion and Recon Application was capable of pumping all kinds of psychological disruption to a target: insults based on their specific gangcult, dark intimations of what the subject really felt about some family member and the so forth. This had just seemed unnecessarily basic and crude.

"Yeah, well, I just don't have the hard info," MIRA said cheerfully. For all that the voice issuing from the exterior bullhorn-attachment had been deepened, roughened and masculinized, MIRA "herself" tended to adopt a female persona. That is, a lighter, higher and feminine voice, while still in some subliminal way failing to be human in any way whatsoever.

"Filesearch on the girl throws up nothing, just like all these total blanks, yeah?" MIRA said. "Like someone went through the files and wiped her footprints out. And the guy never left no footprints in the first place – he's just some kid, you know? I'm just playing the law of averages and throwing out some generic insults. I'm having to improvise."

Drexler ran his glance across the display-monitors bolted to the dash of the NeoGen-modified Humvee – or HumGee – parked under mimetic camouflage-netting outside the junker's yard and which was serving as a scratch C&C for the guys inside.

Wireframe topographics of the yard itself, thermograph readouts of the targets in the van overlaid with extrapolated bio-data. Outputs from the microcams of the three wet-operatives inside.

"Don't try to improvise when you don't have the data," he told MIRA. "It just sounds wrong. It doesn't sound like anything a real human would say."

MIRA gave what sounded like a contemptuous little snort – possibly a sound-sample designed to convey that precise effect.

"I'm a sentient-grade AI, chum, even if I occupy the lower end of the scale. You just follow the orders and do the job and come it like a frigging robot. I sound more human and alive than you do, most of the time."

"That's my prerogative, MIRA. You don't have the option."

"Yeah, whatever you say, *boss*," MIRA said with marked cybernetic sarcasm. "And speaking of time, boss, we're well over that deadline I gave the targets. You wanna give the go-word to take 'em out?"

"Do it," Drexler said. "Remember that the package is our top priority. They can do what they like, but only after the package is secure."

"Yeah, yeah, we all know that," said MIRA. "I'm relaying the order to… hang on. Something's up…

"Check the bio-readouts on the girl. Something freaky's going on with the girl and it's – oh my God…"

There was a blinding flash from outside, washing out the Klieg-illumination in the intensity of its glare, and human-sounding or not, that was the last thing MIRA ever said.

SHAFTS OF MAGNESIUM light blasted from the windows and roof-ports of the van, from the rust holes eaten in its sides. Tendrils of electrical discharge arced to the junkyard-compound's generator unit, travelling the leads to which it had been hooked to NeoGen's Kliegs and exploding them in a shower of sparks.

Vestigial petrochems left in tanks out in the junk piles spontaneously ignited; the tanks detonated. The junk began to burn. The van itself exploded – torn apart by forces within it that were not entirely physical.

And something dark burst from it. Something dark in a wholly different sense than a mere absence of cast light.

Something big. Something shrieking. Something coming now.

5.

IN A PLACE that has no name, a place indefinable in spatial or temporal terms – or for that matter, any terms that might apply to organic matter, let alone life – something vast and inimical and unknowable stirred.

Something was calling to it. Something had made a small fracture in the world. A tiny imperfection, to be sure, but one that could be worked upon. Something that could be forced further apart, with time. If time had any meaning, of course, for this vast and inimical and unknowable thing, which it didn't. It had an eternity in which to operate, after all.

It would be a mistake to believe that the subsumation and destruction of all we know would be anything more than a light snack to this vast and inimical and unknowable thing. The equivalent of a quick pack of potato chips between real meals.

Then again, potato chips come in a variety of interesting flavours, and a pack of them is just the thing to hit the spot. When you're feeling peckish – as the vast and inimical and unknowable thing decidedly was.

For the moment, though, it was in the position of having worked the pack open just enough to insert a finger. Just enough, if it inserted

*the smallest extremity of itself into the world of men, for a small taste.
And this it had proceeded to do...*

HALF-BLINDED AND gibbering with terror, Eddie Kalish scrambled through the junk piles, trying to catch his bearings. Things had shifted around, of course, during the time he had spent away, but Little Deke's had never been what you might call a roaring concern. Things, for the most part, had tended to stay where they were put; Eddie still had some idea of the layout. That was an advantage.

That was, in fact, the only advantage he might have over the people out here in the dark. People and, of course, the... *thing* out here in the dark.

"OH YES, THERE'S something I can do," Trix Desoto had said, eyes a kind of burning black behind the slatted light, "and I'm going to do it now."

She had ripped her hands from the hole in her stomach, trailing strings of some viscous substance that hadn't quite seemed even organic, let alone something that a human body could produce. A mass of this stuff seemed to have clotted in her wound, tendrils of it forming and intertwining and pulsing of its own accord.

The hands had seemed bigger – impossibly bigger, like those anatomical models where the limbs and extremities are distorted to a size comparable to the area of the brain controlling them. The nails had elongated to the point of talons.

Trix Desoto had run one of these claws down her face – for an instant Eddie had thought that she was trying to claw her own eyes out in agony, but instead the tip of a talon had run gently down the side of her face, cutting a slit from the inside of which something glowed like embers in some long-banked fire.

"Run," she had told him, face deadly serious and positively demonic in the light from the slit she had made. A talon had jabbed in the direction of the pale form of the comatose old guy. "Take him and *run*."

All reasonable thoughts about armed NeoGen troops waiting out there in the junk years had vanished – indeed, it was as if all reasonable thought had shut down. The monster snarls and you just run for the tree line or the cave. He had leapt from the van without question and headed for the junk piles.

It was only after the explosion had washed over him, miraculously failing to spear him with flying debris, that he realised that he had unthinkingly followed Trix Desoto's order and taken the body of the old guy with him. It must have been her tone of voice.

Now, EDDIE KALISH decided, the old guy was just dead weight. He left the inert form sprawled by a pile of rotting tyres, gently seeping from the punctures left from being unceremoniously hauled from the med-units.

Off to one side, through the junk, there was a single muzzle-flash and the complete lack of sound from an expertly silenced gun – though any sound of gunfire would have probably been drowned out, in any case, by the high-pitched scream and the sounds of tearing flesh. Whatever it was that Trix Desoto had turned into, it was having a ball.

Or possibly two, Eddie thought, and then really wished that he hadn't.

Eddie moved on, crept around a vaguely familiar heap of panel-sections – and ran straight into one of the surviving NeoGen troops.

Eddie Kalish would never know how lucky he was, in that instant – luck that had been brought about by the confluence of three main factors. The first being that the trooper was currently packing hi-explosive shells into his big MultiFunction Gun.

This would have been singularly *unlucky*, of course, had not one Commander Thomas Marlon Drexler ordered that minimum necessary force be used until the object of their operation be secure. A single hi-ex round fired into the van would have exploded it in much the way that it just had, so the MFG was currently slung over the trooper's shoulder and out of instant reach.

The second factor was that, unlike that produced by conventional explosives, the detonation of the van had released a variety of localized electromagnetic pulse that had knocked out the trooper's infrared night-sight. He was in the midst of tearing it angrily from his face and blinking his eyes to acclimatise to the sudden darkness when he caught the moving silhouette of Eddie.

This lag in reaction-time gave Eddie Kalish the bare second he needed to let out a yip of fear and lurch back – and this was when the third factor came into play, in the form of the heap of panel-sections that Eddie himself had somewhat inexpertly stacked some years before.

These had come, predominantly, from the hulking shells remaining from automobiles of the 1950s and 60s – from before oil embargos and the like had made sheer weight an issue. They were good, solid steel plate as opposed to membrane-thin aluminium that turned to lacework at the first breath of an oxyacetylene torch.

They were an incompetently stacked accident waiting to happen, basically – and now they came crashing down on the trooper.

The screams before, and as, they hit sounded a little odd to Eddie and it was a moment before he worked out why. For some reason, Eddie realised, he'd had trouble imagining a quasi-military stealth-killer as a girl, for all that there was no reason in the world why not.

From the image that terror had etched onto his eyes, though, he now recalled that the shape under the combat-fatigues had been undoubtedly female, and damn well-built at that.

Of course, any shape she might be in now would be decidedly unattractive and quite beside the point. This was the first person Eddie had actually killed in his life, whether by accident or design. He really didn't know how he felt about that.

There was another explosion of sound and light. It seemed that it was coming from beyond the compound wire, and that was just like as to fine with Eddie Kalish. Too much had happened. His reflexes were shot.

All he wanted to do at this point was crawl away somewhere and hide and let the world go to Hell in any way that it liked.

THOMAS MARLON DREXLER slapped at the inert monitors bolted onto the dash and said: "Fuck you you piece of shit!"

This was, in actual fact, the longest single string of expletives he had ever used. He had simply, somehow, never seen the point or felt the need, even in the heat of combat. He was a little surprised that he even had it in him.

The EMP from the explosion within the targets' RV had knocked out the HumGee's electrical systems. MIRA "herself" was probably still alive – or, at least, sentient-grade self-aware – since her housing was rated as shielded for anything up to a pony-bomb nuclear blast.

The secondary systems that would make her being alive and aware of any actual use, however, were blown.

These included the door mechanisms. Drexler had remained here, trapped, while things had exploded outside. He had attempted to work out what was happening in the junkyard compound beyond the wire, but the loss of Klieg-illumination had left him with nothing useful to see.

It was the sense of disassociation from the world that was the worst thing, he vaguely realised. MIRA might have snidely called him a robot, but the fact was that a large proportion of Thomas Marlon Drexler's self-image resided in the fact that he considered himself, basically, a tool.

He was a part of something larger and more important than himself. He was the strong right hand – no, rather the hammer in that strong right hand – when his NeoGen masters required the application of direct force.

This was his function, and he performed it without ego or self-congratulation, without compunction or remorse. Taking out the ringleaders of a labour-dispute, removing some intra-corporate rival together with his wife and kids, it made no odds. It was his function. This was the core of his being and his life.

Now he was stuck here, sealed off from the world and unable to affect it in any way. He was about as much use as a spare dick – and the sensation was maddening.

This was not, quite simply, what the world was and how it worked. It was almost enough to make him take the ten-gauge from where it was stowed under the dash and use it to just switch the world off.

Something big and heavy thumped into the HumGee outside, rocking it on its suspension and flinging Drexler forward to smack his head against the padded crash-cage which – had the electrics been working – would have ordinarily racked itself down on servos to cushion the impact.

This direct evidence of a world outside galvanised Drexler and his basic impulses took over. Now he grabbed the ten-gauge, pulling it free from its snaplocks with no thought in his head save to aim it at the HumGee's windshield and blast his way out.

The fact that the shot would have almost certainly rebounded from the impact-tempered glass and shredded him where he sat was beside the point – the mindless need to simply *act*, overwhelming as it was, had burned away any last vestige of rational thought.

Thus it was that when the entire top of the HumGee split open under a claw and inhuman strength, Drexler was already in the process of bringing up the gun and unloading both barrels.

The shot tore into the thing beyond, opening up a hole within which internal organs gave off their own pale glow.

In this light – or for that matter any other – these organs looked like the insides of nothing on or of this Earth.

For a moment, the creature recoiled, eyes rolling down to regard the wound and jaw yawning open in a moment of imbecilic, even comical, puzzlement.

"Got you, motherfucker," Drexler snarled, thereby increasing, again, the number of times he had sworn in his life by an actually measurable percentage. "Fuckin' *hurt* your ass!"

The moment of incongruous puzzlement passed. The skin of the creature liquefied and flowed over the hole and knitted.

The creature brushed at itself momentarily, and somewhat fussily, with a claw.

Then it reached in, clamped its talons around Drexler's head and hauled him out of the HumGee, snapping his neck in the process.

This was probably more fortunate than otherwise for Thomas Marlon Drexler, since it meant that he could not feel what the creature did next.

From his immobilised point of view, past the foreground spray of various fluids as the creature went to work with a vengeance, Drexler could see the night sky. The stars burned brightly, in a wide range of colours due to suspended atmospheric pollutants.

The last thing Drexler saw was one of the stars visibly move and expand. Something coming.

Big light coming down.

"OH SHIT," EDDIE muttered, increasing the number of times he had sworn in his life by no particular increment at all. "Here comes the backup."

Hunched up in the lee of a caterpillar-treaded hoist, which he had operated years before under the instruction of Little Deke, life had become quite simple, containing a grand total of two possibilities. Either the thing that had once been Trix Desoto would tire of amusing itself with the NeoGen troops and come sniffing after him, or NeoGen reinforcements would arrive to shoot him in the head.

The latter, it seemed, would be the case.

The big VTOL carrier hung in the air stitching fire into the junkyard. Eddie had scrambled for cover before realising that the VTOL was merely firing tracer-flares to provide snapshot-illumination, maybe for some variety of photosensor-system. This inference gave him no impetus to come *out* from cover, though, on account of (a) a direct hit from a tracer-flare wouldn't do him much good, and (b) the little fact that if NeoGen saw him they were gonna shoot him in the head.

As the carrier banked and descended, however, Eddie caught sight of the illuminated logo on its side:

gentech

This wasn't reinforcement for the bad guys, Eddie Kalish realised belatedly. This was the cavalry.

A drop-hatch opened and a score of impact-armoured troopers hit the dirt. Each of them toted a big MFG, and it would have been more to Eddie's taste if they hadn't looked more or less identical to the NeoGen operatives he had seen, but then you can't have everything.

One of them, presumably the squad-leader, carried a small flatscreen readout, which he was busily consulting.

"*Primary target is forty metres south-southeast,*" he ordered through a miniature amplifier. "*Carter and Trant, secure the package.*"

A pair of troopers peeled off and headed in the direction that Eddie vaguely remembered leaving the comatose old guy.

"*Track-and-tranque detail, see if you can't find the silly bitch. Try to take her alive. Try and shock her into latency. The rest of you clean up the area. Standard track and pop…*"

Eddie decided that, on the whole, it would probably be better if he made his presence known rather than wait for the troops to come across him. Moving slow and trying to make himself look as unimpressive and unthreatening as possible, which wasn't hard, he walked from the cover of the hoist and gave the troops a small wave. "Hey, guys ..?"

Those of the squad who remained here, maybe ten in all, swung their MFGs toward him instantly.

"*You!*" the squad-leader bellowed. "*Give me your clearance!*"

"What?" said Eddie.

"*Security key-code clearance! Now!*"

"What the fuck?" said Eddie.

Automatic fire from maybe three sources stitched into him, and that was the last thing Eddie Kalish remembered.

Second Quadrant
Section in the City

FROM BEHIND ME a roscoe belched "Chow-chow!" A
pair of slugs buzzed past my left ear, almost nicked my
cranium. Mrs Brantham sagged back against the pillow
of the lounge… she was as dead as an iced catfish.

"Veiled Lady"
Spicy Detective
October 1937

supplementary data

THE CONURBATION THAT would eventually become known simply as the San Angeles Sprawl was built on the processes of overexpansion and of dying back, both happening simultaneously.

That isn't the oxymoron it might first appear. Population-pressure had been well along the way of thickening up the developments along the routes forming an irregular and somewhat elongated triangle formed by Los Angeles, San Bernardino and San Diego, turning any last vestiges of natural landscape into an urban-landscape, when the ultimate collapse of petrochems as a global source of power had forced human populations to collapse and congeal in a specifically structural manner.

The vast majority of the urban population now subsisted in what were basically corporate hives – fortified and monolithic compound-blocks, resource-regulated and microclimatically controlled, amongst the rubble and wreckage of what was almost literally, now, an urban jungle.

It was, in a sense, as if humanity itself had split itself in two. Those with the ant-like temperament to survive in

corporate-controlled culture had holed themselves up in these arcologies; those who were essentially nomadic, or indeed bandits, took to the roads... but when the world splits in two, whatever the sense, there are always those who fall through the cracks.

Sometimes these people gravitated toward settlements, like the ill-fated Las Vitas in New Mexico, and eked out a living on sufferance, servicing those who truly lived out in the wide-open spaces on the simple basis that there has to be somebody who does.

For the most part, though, they ended up crawling through the tenebrous wreckage of cities cannibalised and consolidated into the corporate hives, living in the ruins of the No-Go Zones. Living the best they could, like maggots on the rotting corpse of the old world.

Of course, even amongst the society of maggots on a corpse, or any other parasite or scavenger, there were differing degrees of devolvement and ferality.

There are some who wax fatter than others... and some who don't.

These had once been the tunnels of the Los Angeles Transit Authority Subway. Never particularly well-regarded or frequented when they had been operational in the first place, years of dereliction had left them choked with the recycling detritus of the ruins and their punctuating corporate compound-blocks above.

Things lived down here in the mix of garbage and toxic sludge, some of them human, some of them not.

A variety of okapi, for example, released by animal rights activists years ago from the Los Angeles City Zoo, had managed to gain purchase here. Turned nocturnal in this endless subterranean night, surviving while all manner of other released creatures died, subsisting on the fronds of a similarly incongruous fungus that had proliferated through the tunnels on escaping from some or other biolab in the world above. Such coincidental survivals might give the more thoughtful pause for thought on the indomitability of biological life.

Not in the case of this particular okapi, though. As it delicately finished its fungus-frond meal and prepared to leave, a meticulously sharpened blade that had once served as one half of a pair of garden shears sliced through its neck and it fell.

Dogboy Who Waits yanked the blade back on the nylon lanyard knotted to the little hole on the tine, which had once served to secure a polypropylene handle. The lanyard itself consisted of woven lengths of fishing line. Dogboy Who Waits, of course, had not the slightest idea of what the origin of these items was; putting them together like this had just, somehow, felt right.

Dogboy Who Waits wasn't even his real name. Indeed, he had only the barest rudiments of conceptual language. He merely knew, in some basic nonverbal sense that he was a Boy, that he felt akin to what he knew as a Dog, and that Waiting was one of the things he did most of. He had been lying patiently in wait for his prey, under the cover of a discarded maintenance pallet, for what those who reckon time in the usual sense would reckon more than thirty-six hours.

Such people who reckoned time would also consider Dogboy Who Waits as maybe fourteen years old, but of course he didn't think in those terms. He was simply there and alive in the faintly fungus-phosphorescent dark that was all he had ever known.

Now the time had come for movement and speed, even urgency. It would not be long before others sensed and smelled the kill.

Working quickly with his blade, Dogboy Who Waits gutted the okapi, identified those lights that were best to eat by touch and wolfed them down. This was the quick nutrition that needed no cooking. Then he began the less hasty business of jointing the carcass and laying up the choicest cuts of hock and haunch in his salt sack.

The kill had been an adult, and large enough that Dogboy Who Waits could countenance leaving some proportion of it for others; the impulse to claim it all and defend it to the snarling death was surmountable. And this was fortunate,

because torchlight was winding its way cautiously through the debris strewn through the tunnels.

As the torches drew closer, Dogboy Who Waits recognised those who were holding them: three boys of roughly his own age, a slightly younger girl trailing behind. A stable and viable breeding-group – insofar as stability and viability had any meaning down here in the tunnels. An actual tribe.

And to the extent that he could know anybody, Dogboy Who Waits knew them, and knew their rituals.

The leader of them – of middle-size, but with the alert look of one who led by resource rather than by means of sheer, mere physical bulk – grunted in what passed for the sub-language peculiar to his tribe, and gestured with his torch to the small pile of entrails which Dogboy Who Waits had, with some consideration, left to one side when butchering his kill.

It is possible that some practices and rituals are basic to human beings, ingrained and dormant in the backbrain and only resurfacing when some imposed and overall patina of "civilization" is absent. On the other hand – and far more plausibly – people just do stuff. All kinds of stuff.

People do certain things in the past and then, quite by chance, they'll do something similar a thousand years later. It's just what people do.

In any case, it just so happened that this particular tribe had evolved an interpersonal ceremony in common with that of plains-dwelling Indians from several centuries before. The leader of the tribe planted his torch in the accumulated mulch of the tunnel floor.

Dogboy Who Waits picked up the entrails, and slowly drew them through the flame. The partially-digested fungus within cooked with a strangely pleasant small, like frying mushrooms.

Dogboy Who Waits and the leader of the tribe hunkered down, facing each other. Each took an end of the length of cooked intestine in their mouths, and then they began to swallow. And swallow. And swallow until their faces were no more than inches apart.

Now would come the actual test of strength – and Dogboy Who Waits had the uneasy feeling that he didn't have it in him. Or, rather, that he had too much. He was beginning to wish that he hadn't filled up on fresh lights after making his kill.

Dogboy Who Waits risked a glance at the other two members of the tribe, the boy and the girl, who were watching the contest expectantly, hungrily. They might fall on him in anger if they saw him cheat – but it was certain they would fall on him, and tear him limb from limb, if he lost.

Dogboy Who Waits decided to risk it, and do what the leader of the tribe, immured in ritual to the point where doing so would never so much as occur to him. He bit down hard on the length of cooked intestine in his mouth and heaved…

AND LATER.

Dogboy Who Waits clambered over a twisted mass of scaffolding and swung himself up onto the sagging remains of what had once been a maintenance gantry. From here it was a clear run to the place he called, in his nonverbal way, home – a ruptured and ketone-reeking tank that had once fuelled the electrical back-up generators of a Transit Authority depot.

The tribe had tracked after him, angrily, for the better part of half a mile, but there had been a sense of squabbling half-heartedness about the pursuit. Their leader had, after all, suffered a lapse in authority – he might have lost the ritual contest by way of trickery, but he had still lost. He might not end up with the others falling on him and tearing him limb from limb, in much the same way as they would have done to Dogboy Who Waits, but the sense of dissention had given Dogboy Who Waits the edge he needed to escape.

Now Dogboy Who Waits made his way along the gantry, senses alert for the slightest evidence of movement or danger – and all unaware that others were hunting, waiting in a manner that would put his own skills to shame…

The explosion set Dogboy Who Waits on fire and knocked him from the gantry to fall thirty feet and hit a loose pile of garbage and concrete scree crumbled from the tunnel walls.

Free hydrocarbons, produced over years by the decomposing garbage, briefly and fitfully ignited under the body's immolation.

The pain was immense, impossible to bear – and then it was simply gone. It had reached the point of overload, where the neurosystem could not recognise it as such. Dogboy Who Waits lay sprawled on the rubble and smouldering garbage, breathing in flame. The mucus in his lungs converted instantly to steam, expanded catastrophically in his lungs and burst them. In the salt-sack slung from his body, choicest cuts of nocturnal okapi meat roasted merrily alongside his own.

"Aw, *fuck!*" came a somewhat irritated voice to one side. "Why'd ya have to use an incendiary round, Karl? Is there any way we can at least save the fuckin' head?"

radio none

"This is WWAXZY News, every hour, on the hour – sponsored by Balls of Joy Premium-brand Profiteroles. Mm-*mm*. Just taste that creamy biotextured soy-milk goodness! Balls of Joy is a property-division of GenTech Industries SA and Creamy Goodness is a registered trademark. All rights reserved.

"And our top story is, of course, that Freak-E has officially announced her split, both romantically and professionally, from manager, Slee-Z. In an official statement she said: 'You nothing but a scrub, Slee-Z. All you ever done is cash in on my talent, motherf____r. Well you can kiss my round black a__ if you think you ever gonna make another cent out of me. I'm Big Master X's b___h now. Word to your motherf_____g mom!'

"The rest of Freak-E's statement is unfit even for broadcast on this station but highlights included allegations that Slee-Z has one of the world's largest collection of porcelain teapots and isn't adverse to the use of a strap-on when it comes to bedroom fun.

"Big Master X is CEO of Big Black Beats Inc and a self-made multi-billionaire. Born in the Brooklyn No-Go in 2007,

Big Master X – real name Justin Jones – overcame the combined handicaps of having a pronounced stutter, being massively obese and hitting every branch of the ugly tree when he fell out of it, to record his first number one single by the time he was nine. The following year he set up his own record label and within six months accepted an eight-figure offer from Eidolon Corp to buy out Big Black Beats. Freak-E is the latest in a string of female recording artists signed to BBB with whom Big Master X has been romantically linked following high profile affairs with Russian teen rap sensation Ivana Sukayov and all three members of Afghan agit-pop trio, Bombs Not Burkas.

"Slee-Z was unavailable for comment but sources close to the music, clothing and prostitution mogul have told this station that Slee-Z is unlikely to take Freak-E's defection, especially to his biggest rival, lying down.

"In other news, aspiring Independent presidential candidate, William Hicks, has announced that he has proof that the information linking the Democratic Confederation of the Congos with the Basque Reunification cell who took out the Washington Memorial last spring to be entirely fabricated.

"What kind of President, asks Hicks, could be so addled and opportunistic as to confuse two entirely different and separate world powers purely on the basis that he considers them both to be dangerous foreigners with guns?

"A White House source, speaking off the record, sez: 'William Hicks might once have had a first-class mind, but these latest statements show that he's now completely delusional – delusion evidenced by his belief that he could ever become President in any real world.'

"And if the independent candidate is delusional then it looks like these things are catching. We here at WWAXZY have been receiving some very strange reports today.

"In Tokyo, more than a hundred subway commuters have spontaneously developed symptoms consistent with that of a Sarin attack. Physical traces of any kind of contaminant has yet to be found.

"The images of ghost-like and gigantic women have been glimpsed floating over several of the world's most isolated communities, variously described as resembling the Angel of Mons, Winged Victory of Samathrace and, in the New Hegonomy of Bangkok as that of Rati, Ragalata the vine of love, Kelikila the Shameless, Mayarati the Deciever – a multiple deity currently appearing in her aspect of a huge-breasted woman who drives all who might behold her mad with carnal lust. To which, all WWAXZY can say, is that some godless savages get all the luck.

"And speaking of massive goddesses who drive all who might behold them mad with carnal lust, we now return you to our back-to-back marathon of Freak-E hits. Here's the hot new mix of 'Be My Pimp'…"

6.

HE WAS:

Caught and killed and falling through darkness, tumbling head-over-heels with his heart in his mouth; boogiemen in the dark, their juju light shining bright behind the ragged holes of their eyes; still he continued to fall and it was heard to breathe... razor-shards in his lungs and blood on the walls and sick, slick mucus on the walls and something was happening to his—

He was:

Plunging through a cavern of membrane, tubular clusters of matter clinging to the sides and small lights flashing among them in a manner reminiscent of readouts. Here and there the membrane walls were ripped open to expose a darkness in which hideously distorted images of human faces were projected: white circles with black-circle eyes and screaming yaws of mouths.

His:

Skin felt loose and gelid. Without pain it sloughed off from his bones and streamed behind him as he fell and (sloughing and reforming, hauling itself back in and tangling, twisting around, transmuting into something bright, so bright, and metametallic that he...)

He:

Hit the floor of the cavern headfirst. Again, there was no pain, merely the abrupt cessation of motion. He lay there for a moment, face buried in a soft and decomposing mulch of what might be meat – or the idea of meat – then hauled himself up.

The skeletal remains of hands attached to forearms sprouted from the fleshy cavern floor, rotted to bone that was a bright and absolute white – far whiter than any bone one might encounter in any real world. The hands were shrouded in a haze of branching microtubular filaments – it was as if something had rotted the flesh away with such peculiar precision as to leave the neural matter intact.

The hands moved. They clutched and scrabbled at him, grabbing at him with a cloying intimacy that seemed to slide around inside his head. Something hot and clotted bursting in his *head*…

And he:

Screamed. Screamed so hard he thought his lungs might painlessly burst. And from him came a Big Light – like a reflex-sting, a burst of white-hot plasma, blasting the clutching hands away from him and burning them to nothing.

He:

For a moment he stood in the smoking crater of charred meat, staring ahead dumbly. After a while he realised that he was holding his hands in front of his face, realised what he was looking at: mirror-bright, his hands were, his whole body was, as though sculpted from solid but nevertheless in some sense fluid chrome.

The sense of cool air on his face.

The explosion of plasma that had come from him had ripped a hole in the membrane-wall of the cavern. Bright light came from it, bright shapes moved beyond.

Feet slipping in grease, crunching on the burned remains of clinging hands, Eddie Kalish walked towards the rip.

"THERE YOU GO. That's a boy!"

Eddie Kalish opened a bleary eye to see something he had never seen before.

Well, he had, but the transformation of it was of such a nature that it left the pattern-recognition areas of the mind temporarily wrong-footed.

When you thought of Trix Desoto, you thought of her in a comedy-nurse costume, wounded, close to death – and about to turn into some diabolical monstrosity from the very lowest reaches of Hell. If Hell actually existed, of course, which of course it didn't.

Looking at her sitting there, now, on the edge of the hospital bed, relaxed and cheerful in an underwired patent-leather catsuit that would do wonders for the self-esteem of any girl, and so on Trix Desoto contrived to be spectacular, it took the mind a moment to adjust.

"Now, my advice to you," said Trix Desoto, "would be to get the 'what happened' and 'where am I' out the way with the minimum of fuss. Everybody tries to find a new way of saying it, and it never works."

Eddie looked blearily around the room. Some part of him vaguely expected it to be a sterile environment, white-tile walled and lit by harsh and buzzing fluorescent tubes. Instead, it was just the kind of neat little room you might find in an expensive private nursing home called Sunny Gables or the like. Plaster walls and cornicing. Drapes over the window. Discreet little oil-pastel landscapes dotted around.

(And it would only be later, much later, that he would finally work out what had been wrong with this. It was simply that the very idea of "A private nursing home called Sunny Gables" would have never occurred to him in his real life. It was simply not in his mental lexicon. Somebody, or something, must have actively put it into his head.)

At the time, though, the room just seemed prosaic and comforting. This was probably to offset the tangled horror of the items that were currently plugged into him, by way of tubes and what appeared to be actual electrical flex.

The med-units seemed to be some hybrid mix of the inorganic and decidedly *organic* – hearts and livers held in steel and polycarbon rack-cages, stimulated by servo-motors and

pumping liquids which, by the colour, could be anything except saline fluid and blood.

The units seemed to twitch and fibrillate, like insects with their carapaces split open and their insides laid out.

"The fuck ..?" Eddie Kalish managed to croak at last. "Wh' happened? Fuck am I?"

"You see?" Trix Desoto said with a small smirk. "Nobody *ever* finds a new way of saying it."

She stood up with a creak of patent leather. The catsuit covered her belly and midriff, but was sufficiently tight and clinging for Eddie to see that the flesh under it was flat and toned, no sign of a wound of any kind.

The ragged and blood-matted hair that Edie remembered from the van in New Mexico now fell in platinum-blonde curls that suggested regular washing in a rejuvenatingly herb-steeped stream next door to a chemical plant.

Trix Desoto crossed the room, with quick scissor-steps, and activated a wall panel by the door. "He's awake now. You can come in." Then she turned to regard Eddie with a not unkindly smile.

"You're safe enough, in the relative scheme of things," she said to him. "We're in the San Angeles Sprawl, in a GenTech facility. Welcome to the Factory."

The door slid open, and a Suit came in.

That wasn't mere colloquial hyperbole. The Suit was a dead and perfect black so that, for example, if an arm was laid across the chest, it was impossible to see the distinction between them; you could only see the Suit in one-piece silhouette.

Protruding from the neck of the Suit, by means of the usual human arrangement, was the neatly groomed head of a man – and once again, neatly-groomed was not mere hyperbole. The hair and beard were cropped and shaped in a manner so precise that one could imagine it having been done follicle by follicle, by micromanipulator, under the direction of a team of design consultants, in an operation costing tens of thousands of dollars.

The effect, however, was somewhat spoilt by the fact that there are some men who simply cannot carry off cropped hair

and beards. And there are some men, frankly, who are con-genitally unsuited to waiting a suit. Or even a Suit.

Later, Eddie would learn that the ensemble was basically a uniform, the standard outfit for GenTech field-management of a certain level – and you damn well wore what was given to you – but for the moment the main impression was a little like that of a child somewhat ineptly dressing up.

This new arrival in the Suit grinned at Eddie – a little shiftily, Eddie thought. The effect might have been due, though, to the black wraparound shades that gave no idea whatsoever of what the eyes might be doing underneath them.

"So you're our mystery wonder-boy," he said, leaving no doubt that *wonder-boy* actually meant: *some little squit I don't particularly give two shits about.* "Eddie, is it? Eddie Kalish? Doesn't quite seem to *fit* with anything, if you get what I mean. Doesn't fit right with where you were. Where we found you. Where does it come from?"

Eddie shrugged, rattling a couple of tubes.

Far as he could recall, that was just always what he had been called. He had simply never thought about it. And he certainly wasn't going to start thinking about it now at the behest of this individual, who he was already beginning to dislike intensely.

(And just when and where, he would wonder later, had he started thinking in terms of this "behest of individual"crap?)

The man shrugged himself, utterly unconcerned rather than sullen. The matter was simply not worth bothering about.

"Call yourself whatever you want," he said. "What do I care? You can call me Masterton – and I'll tell you right now that's not what you might call my real name. That, you'll never know. The important thing is… do you read at all, Eddie?"

"I can read," Eddie Kalish said, shortly. He was getting seri-ously tired of this guy Masterton's somewhat overly familiar manner. "I can write words, too."

Masterton sighed.

"Good for you," he said." What I meant was, do you read many actual books. No? Well colour me surprised.

"In any case, in a lot of books, you get what they call exposition. Some guy tells you what's been happening and what is going to happen. He might be lying like a bastard, and making it up off the top of his head, but the point is that he makes it all hang together and makes it work. He tells you what to do, and what you're gonna do next.

"I want you to think of me as your *exposition*, Eddie, yeah? I'm the one who tells you what you're gonna do.

"Now, a little while back you blundered in on the retrieval operation we were running on Ms Desoto here, and the package she was transporting. You didn't know what you'd got into, and you certainly didn't know any command-identification codes, so our guys just shot you to hell and back. Shot you dead. You're dead.

"Fortunately for you, being dead isn't quite the handicap it once was. We here at GenTech have the technology. We can rebuild, and all that happy crap. Resurrection-and-regen processes courtesy of the good Doctor Zarathustra. It's one of the things we do… and the conditions happened to be right for us to do it to you.

"Now at this point, Eddie, you must be thinking: gee, wow, what's so special about *me* that I get the Zarathustra treatment? Well, let me tell you, you're goddamn nothing. You're just some sorry sap who happened to be on the spot. The upshot of that, what with all the expense and all, is that we now *own* your sorry ass. You're just stone cold nothing and we get to do what we like with you."

Eddie Kalish realised that Masterton had stopped talking, and was just grinning at him in the manner of one having successfully completed a recitation. There was an air, indeed, that he had been subjected to a polished and often-repeated spiel.

Off to one side, he noticed, Trix Desoto was watching him, too, with a sense of expectation. Eddie wondered how many times they had put someone in this situation, whether they had a bet on how he would now react.

Well, screw 'em, frankly. Eddie wasn't going to give them the satisfaction of any reaction at all. He just looked dumbly

down at himself – and for the first time caught sight of his own body. In this he was aided, in that it was covered with a slightly cloudy but mostly transparent polythene sheet, rather than a bed sheet.

People tend not to consciously examine their own bodies without some external impetus in the manner of, for example, pain. This is for the simple reason that – barring the obvious effects of working out, or having an arm lopped off by a rotary saw or the suchlike – there are certain fundamentals that the mind absolutely refuses to recognise might change.

Now Eddie Kalish stared down at himself, positively goggle-eyed, as rafts of certainty broke apart and sank behind his eyes. "Jesus fucking *Christ!*"

Off to one side Trix Desoto smirked maliciously.

"That's a fin you owe me, Masterton," she said.

7.

He was in:

A limitless, deprisensory gulf, strung though with bright tendrils of some drifting gas that seemed to twist and curl in on itself resolving itself into discrete and dislocated images. Lantern fish of the bulbously misshapen sort one finds in ocean trenches, twisted so that the mouths of comedy-and-drama-mask faces yawned on their flanks; the masked face of a surgeon, a light clipped to his temple blazing as a scalpel flashed across it; the sliced and encrusted remains of some horse-like creature, with two heads, wrapped within rusting coils of razorwire; an antique roll-top desk with something horrible inside; snipping windshield and a hole under the wall and the red wet razors sliding soft inside the...

All of this was:

Background. All of it. He drifted through it feeling the actual physical slicing of something sharp-edged flowing in his head; drifted from the slit he had made and the red wet tunnel and those cloying skeletal hands...

It was some time before he realised that he was flying.

* * *

EDDIE KALISH JERKED awake, under his transparent polythene sheet, dream-images still crawling through his head. There was definitely something happening in there, something inside actually shifting into some new alignment.

He couldn't escape the feeling that, somewhere in their narrative, the dream-hallucinations were actually trying to *tell* him something. Something was being downloaded into him, the nature of which at this point he could not quite grasp.

Well, if things were shifting around in his mind, no less inside the body on the bed in this twee little hospital room packed with insectoid biopacks. You never knew, on waking up, what might have changed: the length of a finger here, the fleshing out of muscle-texture there.

The biorganic implants which had resurrected Eddie's lifeless corpse, kickstarted and maintained his metabolism, Masterton had explained, were now being mimicked and supplanted by the entirely organic Zarathustra processes.

It would be several days before they completed the job, leaving Eddie Kalish in better shape than he had ever been before. Physically stronger, with reflexes and mental faculties enhanced.

Residual processes would greatly enhance his damage-resistance and healing factors, in much that same way that they had allowed Trix Desoto to survive after a gunshot wound that had left half her guts spilling out.

Eddie had asked if he was going to turn into a superman or something because, quite frankly, he had kind of liked the idea of that.

Masterton had snorted, and told him not to be such a tool. The human world was designed and built to human tolerances and dimensions – an actual *superhuman* would be forever braining himself on ceilings and crushing things he tried to pick up. It would be pointless – at least so far as the purposes of GenTech were concerned.

Masterton had suggested, since Eddie was going to spend the next few days lying there and being about as useful as a spare prick, that he orientate himself as to the aims and expectations

of his new GenTech masters by way of the datanet. This Eddie had dutifully done, by way of a wireless display pad found for him by Trix Desoto, and pretty much simply for the sake of having something to do.

Eddie Kalish had never used the datanet in his life, having spent most of it only vaguely aware that such a thing existed. Little Deke had been extremely jealous of his access and had never let him have a look.

It struck Eddie as slightly weird that, given that, he had taken to it so readily. Of course, this might have had something to do with the fact that the datanet, by its very nature, was so simple to navigate that it could be used by a concussed ant – but no, Eddie thought, there was more to it than that.

In some strange way he was able to see the hidden shapes behind the data. Well, alright, it wasn't that he actually *saw* what password-clearance codes were or anything like that; it was just that he was somehow able to make the right moves to get himself inside so-called classified files that he'd decided to have a look at.

It must have been some side-effect of the resurrection implants and the Zarathustra regen-procedures, he thought. The things downloading into his head that he was reacting to in dreams.

Pity he couldn't have had a taste of that before a complete lack of knowing about command-codes had had him shot. Bit of a tautology there, of course, he supposed, but so what?

In any case, it was in this way that Eddie came across a slightly fuller explanation for the Zarathustra processes, currently at work on his own mind and body, than Masterton had given him.

THE BASIS FOR the Zarathrusta processes had come from the "disaster" that had, notoriously, struck the city of Des Moines a decade before – the nature and origin of which had never been satisfactorily explained.

The specific and targeted nature of what came to be known as the Rapture Bug suggested that it had been actively

designed, but no human agency had ever stepped forward to take responsibility for the effect.

Besides, designed or not, the mechanisms of the Bug seemed far in advance of any technology available on planet Earth. Speculations as to some extraterrestrial – or even extradimensional – origin were endless and ultimately fruitless. The simple fact remained that it was as if the Rapture Bug had come from some entirely other world.

Initial investigation of the effect suggested – erroneously – that the Bug had operated by means of nanonetics. In fact, as it was later learned by a process of back-engineering, it operated on the subatomic level: a quantum-level self-propagating construct that, in effect, rewrote the base code of the world. It was designed to target itself upon, incorporate itself within and radically alter the individual, living humanoid form.

Its basic nature meant that when released, it proliferated something like a virus but *instantly* – or at least at the speed of light – saturating its target area in a matter of seconds. The vast majority of those caught within its sphere of influence never even had the luxury of *waking up* to find their world had changed.

The initial effects had been quite impressive to say the least. The pores of every human body opened like industrial vents and began pumping out a sludge and spray of deconstructed pathogen-components and accumulated toxins.

Foreign bodies like artificial hearts, hips or small items lodged in some inextricable location as a child were physically *ejected*, often at velocities of several thousand metres per second. There were cases, in particularly crowded situations, of some largish hunk of matter being *fired* into someone else, ejected in its turn to hit some other body and the process continuing on for up to an hour.

Old scars and fresh wounds healed themselves in a matter of seconds. Calloused tissue went, too, being the product, effectively, of cumulative minor injury – with the result that fingertips and the soles of feet ended up as soft and pink as those of a baby. The Rapture Bug would counter further damage to this otherwise vulnerable new flesh, of course – though unfortunately without suppressing the pain reflex.

The question of biological organ transplants had been somewhat problematic, on the basis that the Rapture Bug was, in the end, something of a misnomer. It did not, as such, resurrect the dead; it merely transformed the living into something effectively immortal and invulnerable.

Hearts, livers, lungs and so forth with a dissimilar genetic coding from their hosts were ejected and replaced, but being living humanoid matter in their own right couldn't die. The "homing" mechanisms of the attendent to the Bug meant that they would gravitate together with the other such items transplanted from the original donor. Piles of living offal, sitting there forlornly and without the ability to regenerate further.

The primary biological transformations that made sexual reproduction instantly obsolete, among the good citizens of Des Moines, had occurred with the same speed as the regeneration of original hearts and lungs and renal systems… with the result that a lot of those actively engaged in copulation at the time ended up being catapulted across the room. Pregnancies spontaneously aborted, the reaction driving several thousand sudden mothers into the air to bury their heads in any available ceiling.

Fortunately, as coherent living humanoid matter, the offspring came under the remit of the Bug and would survive to grow, just as those children whose entrance into the world had been slightly less dramatic.

Twins, though, were and are the worst known cases on record. Or triplets, or quads… those separate human beings, in any case, sharing an entirely similar DNA pattern-signature. With them, the "homing" mechanisms of the Event operated with a vengeance…

AND BETTER, EDDIE thought, to forget about those shrieking, boiling, continually exploding and imploding lumps of matter that were the end result of two, or three, or any number of human-sized objects trying to occupy a single human space. Better to forget the fact that, for all of it, they were still by all accounts alive.

The enhanced insight, the thing inside that let him pull the real meaning out of stories, chose this moment to cut in.

Hadn't it been lucky, Eddie thought that GenTech had been right on hand to throw up containment when the Rapture bug, whatever it was, had hit Des Moines?

Wasn't it just so *fortunate* that this Professor Zarathustra had been able to reverse-engineer, tone down, tweak and reproduce the effect in a manner that was (a) useful to GenTech itself, and (b) resulted in a rejuvenation product that every rich old scum-bag under the sun would be falling over themselves to buy.

It couldn't have worked out better if GenTech itself had loosed the Bug in its prototypically virulent state, using the unfortunate citizens of Des Moines as experimental subjects...

Eddie decided that he'd rather like to learn a bit more about GenTech aims. He was only following Masterton's orders, after all.

A few moments later he had stumbled on the command-codes for the various surveillance cameras dotted around the corridor-complex that Trix Desoto had referred to as the Factory.

There was a security station with its complement of armed guards.

There was a refectory space, and the medical technician – dressed, alas, in a decidedly less exciting manner than had been Trix Desoto in her comedy-nurse costume – who periodically came to administer the sedative hypos that, apparently, were intended to regulate Eddie's sleeping patterns and which worked insofar as they knocked him out like a light.

There was a room remarkably like the one Eddie had imagined on first waking up here – brightly lit and walled with antiseptic while tile. On a surface that looked disquietingly like a mortuary slab lay a thin, pale figure that Eddie recognised: the old guy from New Mexico. The body stirred. Obviously still not dead, then.

A Suited figure instantly recognisable as Masterton was confer-ring with a medical technician Eddie didn't know as she plugged cables into a sensor-unit, suspended on a gimbal-rig over the old guy, and ran the self-diagnostics. Then they nodded together and the technician activated the unit.

Eddie couldn't believe what happened next. Or rather, he believed it... he just wished that he couldn't.

8.

AND FOR A while he:

Didn't feel like doing anything but fly, pinwheeling through the air over the abstract mesh of tendrils, alive to nothing but the rush of kinaesthesia. The simple joy of it.

Eventually, he:

Regained some grip on himself and on his mind; if he was here yet again then is was probably important. There was something his mind was trying to tell him. There was something here for him to learn.

On the extreme edge of perception, he caught a glimpse of:

Creatures of some kind, hanging in the air, sculling lazily through the gulf with cilia-like pseudopodia. Their bumbling course drew them closer to him. They appeared to have noticed him.

He:

Decided to hurry things along and meet them halfway. He was actually, to be frank, some small part of his mind was telling him, getting a bit tired of the obliquity. He wanted to know what this was about once and for all. He rotated himself laterally in the abstract air and accelerated toward the creatures.

As he drew closer, more of the:

Creatures became evident, in tens, and hundreds, thousands… and at last millions. There was a swarm of them. As he drew closer, individual details became distinct – and something inside him began to scream. The same word. Over and over again.

Say it three times and it's true.

A barbed and chitinous hook shot for him, a length of slimy cord trailing in its wake and attaching it to one of the bulbous creature-masses. The hook punched into his horrified and gaping mouth, burrowed through to burst from the back of the neck with a clunch.

The pain was immense; it:

Hauled him, the creature, on its line, towards its mass. In human terms, in waking terms, the bulk of it would have been miles across. A seething chaos of forms and textures that suggested some weird mix of corruption and clockwork, bone cogs and escarpments ticking through a black and churning mass of diseased bile.

The:

Creature hauled him, spinning on his line, into the foetid mass of itself. Buried him inside himself. Engulfed him.

EDDIE KALISH SHOOK himself awake. He had to be awake and ready for this. Like the old joke, it was almost time for him to go to sleep.

At least, it was almost time for the medical technician to come in with the hypo. Eddie had wondered, more than once, what the purpose of it really was; it wasn't as if he didn't spend the days and nights drifting in and out of dreams in any case.

Maybe the staff needed the routine of knowing that there were certain hours when patients were guaranteed to be sparked out.

In any case, the procedure would prove useful now. Eddie spent a minute or two with his datapad, accessing the surveillance systems and keying in a number of commands he knew how to enter like they were written on the back of his hand – without ever quite knowing how he knew them.

Presently, the technician came bustling in. Under her somewhat generic-looking GenTech staff uniform she was a cheerful girl, in her late teens, named Laura Palmer, if you

could believe the little polycarbon plaque clipped to her lapel. To the extent that he have her any consideration at all, as a person, Eddie quite liked her.

"Evening, Mister Kalish," she said cheerfully. "And how are we this evening?"

She always called Eddie *Mister Kalish* with a kind of joking parody of respect, like he was an old guy who kept pissing himself and had to be led around by hand and jollied along. Maybe it was just what the people running hospitals always did with the people in their care – Eddie Kalish had no basis for comparison.

And not that even thinking about the idea of old guys didn't open up a nasty can of worms, for Eddie, at the moment.

"Don't feel well," Eddie mumbled, trying for what he imagined as sounding ill – but succeeding merely in the sort of voice that people used to use when phoning the office on the day of a really important event like the sun being out and feeling like going fishing. And then they cough.

"Feel bad…" Eddie continued, breaking into a cough and waving his right hand randomly and vaguely in an attempt to indicate something about his left shoulder. "Look at this…"

"Don't you worry," medical technician Laura Palmer said, producing the hypo from its ziplock case with cheerful briskness. "A good night's sleep and you'll be right as rain."

Automatically, though, she had leaned in, inclining her head toward the shoulder Eddie had indicated. Eddie Kalish reached up and grabbed her head and smacked her face into the wall.

He'd merely planned to knock her out, but he didn't know his strength. The force of it pulled Laura Palmer physically off her feet to the extent where she literally left one shoe behind.

There was a sharp crunch that Eddie Kalish would subsequently spend years trying to forget and fail. A spray of blood.

The motion had ripped out several of the tubes plugged into Eddie's arm. Now he grabbed the other tubes and contact leads attached to and plugged into him and pulled them off and out. He had no idea what this was gonna do to him,

at this point in whatever Zarathustra procedures were going on, but at this point he didn't give a shit.

Time to move. Time to get the hell *out*. That was all that counted.

He spent a few seconds, though, checking the body of Laura Palmer. He thought he'd crushed her skull, but in the end it seemed that he had merely broken her nose. Her breathing was ragged, and Eddie had no idea of how much he might have hurt her in an ultimate sense, but at least she was still alive as of now.

He fumbled through her uniform until he found the key-card which had given her access to his room, then bundled her up in the polythene sheeting that had so recently covered his own body and left her on the bed, arranging the various tubes and leads so that they might or might not appear to be connected to her. If anyone were to look in, it wouldn't pass even a cursory glance, but what the hell, you never knew.

The anaesthetic hypo lay where Laura Palmer had dropped it, its ziplock case containing several more to one side. Eddie picked them up and got the hell out of there.

EDDIE JAMMED HIS stolen keycard into the slot. A panel readout pulsed from red to amber and the door slid open onto darkness. The faint smell of someone else — and someone, or some thing, that might or might not be entirely human.

Eddie had never, really, been in a room used by a single person as entirely personal space. He had no idea if what he could make out of the contents, in the light spilling from the doorway from the corridor outside, was usual or not.

A scattering of discarded holo-vid disks, data-wafers and actual bound paperback books which must have cost a fortune to whoever had paid for them, decomposing in some abstract sense to informational mulch. Visible titles, in the second-hand light, included: *Briefing for a Descent into Hell, A Cure for Cancer, The Eye of the Lens, The Odyssey, Paradise Lost, The Medusa Seed* — that one quite obviously torn to shreds with some anger, and hurled away with some force — and *Camp Concentration*.

A collection of dolls – or rather, a collection of broadly humaniform figures ranging from proprietary children's toys to an antique, jointed, wooden artist's marionette. Each of these figure had been twisted into postures suggestive of agony, laughter, orgasm, some particular and telegraphic emotional state.

All had been modified in some manner. A stuffed rag doll, for example, had been meticulously skinned with hand-stitched thin black leather. Scrawled in bright pink lipstick across something that looked like a huge egg with diminutive arms and legs stitched on (Eddie had never heard the nursery rhyme Humpty Dumpty) with poppy eyes, stringy hair and an approximation of green velveteen pants, was the word SUCK.

A brightly-keyed technocrome poster of the old movie goddess, Anna Nicole Smith, arching her back in a pose and gold lamé borrowed from the even older movie goddess, Marilyn Monroe.

Mismatched four-colour facial features, ripped from other sources and pasted, turned her smile into something insane and rictive, her eyes burning holes of psychosis.

The sleeping form of Trix Desoto on the somewhat foetid expanse of a mattress. She was half-transformed into… well, whatever the hell it was she transformed into.

Something between a rumble and a growl came from her, in rhythm with sleep-breathing. Something that might or might not have been words. She might or might not be saying the word "mouth", for some reason, over and over again.

In terrified silence, Eddie slipped into the room. Something slithered under his foot – something hard and thin and slippery like the cover of an antique glossy magazine – and for a moment he stumbled, arms pin-wheeling in an attempt to regain his balance.

Something in her alerted by the shift in the air, the partially transformed Trix Desoto stirred and grunted. Then she settled down again.

Somehow, at the expense of crushing a fold of inner cheek between his molars, Eddie preserved his silence. The taste of

fresh blood, The sickening feel of crushed mucus-membrane in his teeth.

At last he made it to the sleeping form. There was an area of skin below her left scapula that looked to be more human than otherwise. So Eddie used his purloined anaesthetic hypo on that.

Trix Desoto's breathing slowed. She relaxed further into sleep. It might have been Eddie's imagination, but he was sure that, for a moment, the transformation of her body had kicked into reverse, leaving her form looking visibly more human.

Last of the brilliant escape-plans, here; a simple case of trading up.

Eddie rooted through the various possessions and clothes on the floor until he found the thing he needed.

There was also a pair of generically nondescript jeans and a shirt, no doubt used when just generally slobbing around, that served at a pinch to fit Eddie due to Trix Desoto's somewhat overstated curves. When in a halfway human form, at least.

The timeclock in Eddie's head — another enhancement courtesy of Prof Zarathustra, he supposed — ticked off the patrol-pattern changes in the guards in the corridors outside. Not particularly good or easy to get past them, here and now, but it wouldn't get any better. It was time to move.

Eddie Kalish went steppin' out.

9.

HE NO LONGER *recalled a specific point of origin. (Some big stone egg spat uterine slick from a fissure in Mount Fuji? Hatched by sun and acid rain; autonomic, anthromythic monkeyman.) The strings of RNA detached and shifted, the meme inside the meat machine supplanting and segueing, supplanting once again like a set of nested cones twisted through Dimension X (where the loathsome cilia-things squatted and watched, at this particular and palsied section of the Millennium, through their fiendish and segmented telescopes) in a recurring and perpetually re-evolving loop. (The canisters were coming.)*

He could no longer remember a name. Not to feel it. He inhabited a world without sequence or names.

And the meat machine like a philosopher's axe; replace the head and change the pole. The same man every time or someone new?

In Barranquilla, in 3017, they had done coca cut with methyl-dex and pigshit 'til hearts stopped cold, sold still-warm suka for the upkeep on their own implants, caught the uplink to the Hook for hypoxia and calcium depletion and polycarbon substrates shot through bone. Convected airborne oestrogen in the geodesics on the Mare Iridium, our swollen glands and our burst and haemorrhaging eyes. Kamo had died there, he recalled. (Kamo who?)

Took the freezer up and out for cryogenic renal shutdown. That was 2434. Took the infra to C7 and it excised the CNS and ate it. Worked the meat rax of the Malay Chain, up on poppers built from Bhopal ketones; in the mouth for food and airspace, up the butt for credit for lymphatic system-swap before the virus went syndromic (I don't recall.) Periodic inert plugs of biomass to plug the minor spirochaetal holes...

If we were to live in these new quasi-spaces, he supposed, we had to leave the very idea of our bodies and our physcal brains behind, shearing off in little dislocated fragments under an abstract accelera-tion, perpetually renewing, a perpetual disconnected death of memory-attrition (of which we are the sum).

And so, at last, after several major refits and a conceptual rebore, after several empty centuries of wandering, the patchwork mariner comes at last again to Eden, a misnomer, where the coffins gawp like open presses. Searching for something lost and gone, that he cannot name but wants. They killed a world, here. Men, I mean. I think. They killed it and they kept on killing it and then they stopped. No big story, no big deal. They just stopped when it was dead.

There are people, obi-people in the wreckage, who restore the mem-ory and thus a name. the price is that everybody dies, the result is that, of course, at some point, everybody comes.

Everyone came back to Planet Earth. At some point. Back to Planet Earth in the past, when it was still there...

TRIX DESOTO CAME across Masterton, in the sparely furnished and vaguely monastic chamber that served him, here in the Factory, as his office and living quarters combined, in the process of flipping through a one-shot disposable LCD data-wafer, of the sort that had entirely supplanted bound paper books in the last decade and a half.

A twentieth-century eye might have been puzzled, insofar as an eye can be puzzled, at a piezoelectric unit being more disposable than paper, but these days it wasn't even an issue. Sand and synthesized chemical crystals were plentiful and cheap. Trees were on the ragged edge of extinction and price-less.

Masterton had a faint and absent sneer on his face that spoke ill of the half-hour to come.

"Do you know, I think it's at this point," he said, confirming it, "that I think the whole intrinsic structure of the thing falls spectacularly apart."

Masterton, Trix knew, had pretensions to being a man of literary sensibilities – and that he sometimes played that up to type. He used it as a petty form of minor torture; pontificating endlessly on the subject of something meaningless and banal when he knew that there was something you were desperate to talk about.

"I mean," he said, tapping the data-wafer meaningfully, "I like a somnambulating prolapse of coruscating bog-postmodernist elliptical prose as well as the next guy, but this is just completely disappearing up its own ass. We now have a grand total of *three* oblique but ultimately ambiguous explanations as to what's going on – alien intervention, interdimensional incursion, and now even *time*-fracture references for fuck's sake – all to explain the big news that some guy meets this girl and they end up screwing. I really do have no idea why I read this crap."

"Masterton…" Trix Desoto said, hoping to God she wasn't sounding apologetic. "We really need to talk about the situation."

"And you can just see how it's all going to end up, right," continued Masterton, seemingly all oblivious. "Our confused and battered and power-imbalanced male-principle guy is gonna end up sorta *merging* in the heat of passion with our dominant but ultimately power-uncorrupted female-principle girl in a million little variegated twinkly lights, there to produce some sort of mythical and metaphorical hybrid; some fabulistic gestalt that – Jesus, but it's all so goddamn old…

"Screw it, let's hunker down. Have you any idea about what it was set Johnny Fucko off?"

"…" For a moment Trix Desoto experienced a clash of mental gears before realizing that Masterton was suddenly back on the job. "Best we can work out," she said, "it was

just a confluence of events. Nothing sinister as such. No outside factors. The certain... peculiarities of his Zarathustra treatments – you know, because of the thing – had him developing his techno-mesh skills well ahead of schedule. This allowed him to get into the systems, and the nearest thing we guess is that he came across *this*..."

Trix Desoto crossed to the playback-monitor on Masterton's desk and punched up a playback. On the screen, the pale figure of an elderly man was in the process of being cut into bloody slices by a laser-cutter unit.

"He wouldn't have known what was happening," Trix Desoto said. "He wouldn't have known that the package was just, in the end, a clone, schematic data cytoplasmically encoded into its neurotecture. He must have thought that this was what we're in the business of doing to, uh, *real* people."

"Well, yeah," said Masterton. "We *are* in the business of doing that sort of thing to real people. The Harvesting programme out there in the No-Go..."

"Granted. But he never got the chance to be acclimatized and indoctrinated. He just rabbited. He took down the med-tech, Laura Palmer–"

"How is our lovely Laura, by the way?" Masterton asked, seemingly all concern. You'd have to know him to realize that he didn't give a shit and was just saying it for the sake of sounding even remotely human.

"Give it some years," Trix said, "and she might be able to eat with something other than a spoon. Anyhow. He took down Laura Palmer, boosted what he thought of as a sedative hypo and her keycard–"

"Which only opens internal doors," said Masterton. "Medical staff aren't permitted to carry anything else for just this reason."

"Right. So maybe he tried the main access hatch with it and then had to rethink, or maybe he knew that in the first place. It's impossible to tell since he blinded the securicams.

"Whatever. He ended up in my quarters. I suppose he really bought the idea that the hypo contained a sedative and just

gave it to me to keep it down – pure luck that it put me down and *out*, you know, because of the thing.

"Then he just picked up my personal keycard – which of course works on the main hatch – and just strolled out. He's out there in the No-Go, now. He could be out there any-where."

"Hmf." Absently, Masterson tapped the pulp-fiction data wafer he had been reading against the edge of his desk. Then he threw it over his shoulder. It hit the wall and shattered into dust.

"Maybe we'll get lucky quick," he said. "Maybe a SAPS squad'll come across him and realize what they have before it's too late.

"In any case, it won't ultimately matter. The second the... peculiarities of his Zarathustra processes go from latent to overt, we'll draw a bead on him the same way we tracked you out there in New Mexico. You know. Because of the thing."

AND IT'S 2914. *An Underlevel backroom in the southern continental colony arcologies, hermetically sealed from the irradiated gravepits. I'm looking and thinking human, now; more human than I've approxi-mated in a while, since the fashion's swung away from it and I like to buck the fashion: ectomorphic, parchment-pale and worn black suit and stovepipe hat. Curled around my neck the remnants of a modi-fied spider monkey, picked up exactly where I can't recall, its remaining flesh desiccated and partially mummified. It can still move, and think, but there's nothing much inside. Other things are here, all entirely unlikely. I think-process they're human, but how does one tell?*

One is human in precise and absolute detail, down to the DNA. An aboriginal, in the present sense, obviously. There are still some left. Her disguise is complete. I'm trading half-hearted favours, secret, sweet and precious with Mine Host's late wife (he laughing fit to bust, a ready chorus, she pendulous and greasy and long-since sloughed and stuffed and mounted).

And she's looking at me 'cross her glass of Soma sunshine (3-methyl-4.5-methylinedioxyamphetamine spiked with strychnine for that little

extra body, natch) with eyes simultaneously dark and flaring, like pol-
ished onyx. A deep one, this; a strata angel, impact-fractured. You can
see down to the animal core.

Change the senses by a conscious act of relay-switching will. You're
male, I think, she said. Have you always been male?

I can't remember. It's true; I can't.

This is all conducted by way of the eyes. One never knows, quite,
how it happens; the transition point between apperception and appre-
ciation; mumbled inanities that remain unmemorable and inane;
tracing tissue hard and arabesqued and hitting something engorged
and slippery (is this mine?).

Mandible-glands extend into the throat, skeening complex and
febrile, pumping a thin sugar-syrup down a gullet that swallows, con-
vulsively, on its sweetness, and something inside fractures...

EDDIE KALISH CAME to in what had once been the restroom of
a Mister Meaty burger franchise.

It was daylight outside, but with the shifting quality of day
moving on towards night. He must have been asleep for hours.

The tenor of his dreams had shifted since busting out of the
Factory, possibly in response to the simple fact of his change
of circumstances in real life.

Something inside was trying to tell him something new. He
tried to remember what the dreams had actually been about.

Eddie took stock.

The face in a surviving scrap of mirror, which had once
covered an entire restroom wall, was pretty much the same as
Eddie remembered, if rather more lined and drawn, and he felt
a bit relieved about that.

He'd had the horrible suspicion that the Zarathustra
processes might resculpt his face into something like that of a
movie star – and while a lot of people would have probably
preferred that, or at least welcomed some slight reduction in
the general rattiness-quotient, then it just wouldn't have been
him anymore.

The body – and Eddie wasn't quite ready to call it *his* body,
yet – was lean and well-toned, certainly not muscle-bound,

which was a bit of another relief on account of how Eddie didn't really feel like coming it with the dickless fuck in a posing pouch.

Premature unplugging from GenTech medical devices did not seem to have affected it unduly. Indeed, the puncture wounds from the unplugging had already healed to small white scars which would themselves fade to nothing in a matter of hours.

There was, however, a vague and crawling feeling in his stomach, which worried Eddie until he realised that he was so hung up on checking for something wrong that he had failed to recognise that he was hungry.

The diner itself was a burnt-out shell, long since abandoned in the general exodus to the corporate compound-blocks and of no use whatsoever to whatever No-Go denizens might remain. There was certainly no food here; it had just been a place to hole up.

EDDIE KALISH HAD gone out through the access-hatch of the Factory expecting to find himself on some floor or other of a compound-block. He'd expected to have to deal with more security systems and corporate uniforms and people demanding to know who he was, what his job was, why he wasn't doing it and then calling for the guards.

They'd have shouted things like "imposter!" and "seize him!", too, in the imagination of one Eddie Kalish.

In fact, he had emerged to find himself in a run-down complex of warehouse-spaces in the wreckage-strewn wasteland of the No-Go itself. Whatever it was that GenTech was doing, here in what they called the Factory, they obviously wanted to keep it at arm's length.

Off to the north – and Eddie had found that something inside him now knew, precisely, which direction Magnetic North actually was – the lights of the multicorporate hives shone.

In the No-Go, lights of a more sporadic and fitful kind burned as those who still lived there went about their nocturnal business.

Eddie's plan, such as it was, had been to simply get out. There was no way he'd ever have worked for GenTech in the first place, and definitely no way for an asshole like Masterton.

Catching sight of the old guy getting sliced to hell and back had just moved his schedule up.

Out here in the No-Go at night, he was entirely out of his element. He hadn't been up for anything more than avoiding the light guard presence in and around the warehouses – GenTech trying to keep attention to a minimum – and look for somewhere to hole up and hide.

Now, in daylight, Eddie Kalish was feeling better. Time to make some actual plans. Find food, boost some transport and just get the hell away.

Spanky reconditioned body and a brain with stuff in it that it didn't have before. Plus you could spot the bad things coming a mile off in daylight – nothing really bad could happen in daylight, right?

Eddie Kalish loped from the shelter of the burnt-out diner, completely unaware of how the flesh on his bones, quite suddenly, slid and pulsed into a new configuration.

He just felt hungry. He needed to eat.

10.

"IT'S GONE OVERT," said Trix Desoto, matter-of-factly, her eyes unfocussed, most of her attention still on operating the tracker.

"This soon?" Masterton was surprised. But not *too* surprised, or he would never have attempted to set up a trace this early in the first place.

"It's a virulent strain," said Trix. "Or maybe it's just general panic-reflex, you know?"

An entire wall of the Factory's intel-and-communications suite was taken up with Tracksat monitors and readouts. The room was packed with tactical-command consoles and general logistically interpolative technology of a sparse and functional, quasi-military design.

Trix Desoto, however, was plugging into a unit of a different kind: a bulbous pod of fleshy matter, its skin of a similar colour and texture as that of a human, which pulsed as though in some self-contained way alive.

Literally plugged. A length of what appeared disquietingly like intestine ran from the pod to her forehead, there to disappear into a socket that looked disgustingly like a sphincter.

Personally, Masterton thought she was showing off; she could just as easily, after all, have interfaced with the tracking pod by laying her hands on it.

"Estimated flip-out into Conversion in three minutes," Trix Desoto said.

"Do you have a vector on him?" Masterton asked. "Where's he going to hit when he flips?"

Trix Desoto rattled off a string of coordinates. Masterton punched them into a console and examined the result.

"Typical," he said wearily. "Just the job. Fun for all the family. Do we have anybody on the ground who can run a stage-one intercept?"

"So what you reckon, Lenny? We made our quota?"

Lenny made a pointed little pantomime of totting up the inventory on his data-pad, and sighed. "No, we haven't made our quota, Karl. We haven't made our quota at all. Would you like to know why we haven't made our quota, Karl?"

"Why haven't we made our quota, Lenny?" asked Karl, a little meekly.

"We haven't made our quota, Karl, because some trigger-happy asshole keeps blowing off people's heads or burning them to shit with incendiary rounds."

"Sorry, Lenny," sad Karl.

For all that the majority of the San Angeles Sprawl lived in the corporate compound-blocks, where such things as food and sanitation and medical services were supplied as a part of that particular deal with the devil of commerce, there were a number of small satellite communities out in the No-Go itself. Pockets of independent and what might, with charity, be called semi-criminal activity, of which the multicorps themselves made use.

Communities of data-hackers, chemical-crackers, an entire and busy sex-industry – people who would never be let inside the compound-blocks in a million years, but to whom were extended an elaborate system of protection and supply. The multicorps needed those people who lived and worked out on

the edges – as a source of innovation, recreation and even in some cases experimentation – so they made at least some effort to keep them alive.

The San Angeles Paramedical Service was, ostensibly, funded by a multicorporate consortium to bring – as the name suggests – paramedical services to those remaining in the No-Go zone. Medical treatment was free… provided you agreed to donate such biological material as might be appropriate, to the organ-banks or for biomedical research, should you be unfortunate enough to die despite the very best of paramedical efforts.

The end result of this was obvious. You didn't call the SAPS in if you were attached to your bodily parts and wanted to stay that way. And if you caught sight of one of their Meat Wagon hovercraft, you rabbited and hid before they could draw a bead on you.

In the violent and casually lethal world of the No-Go, the SAPS, at best, performed the general function of vultures.

"So, you know what I'm thinking, Karl?" said Lenny.

"What are you thinking, Lenny?" said Karl.

"I'm thinking, Karl," said Lenny, "that it's time we had ourselves another little hunting party. Seems that I happen to recall some folks with a small lab not far from here."

"Chemical lab, Lenny?" asked Karl. "Not, uh, a chemical lab doing stuff that might be, you know, important to the Big Guys?" He pronounced the name as though it were significantly capitalized, as indeed it was.

"Nothing of the sort, Karl," Lenny reassured him. "Jerkoffs are strictly retro. They're just brewing up a little line in crystal-meth."

"Just the sort of cowboy operation, Lenny, that could explode from under them at any time…" Karl said thoughtfully. "Total loss of life in a deplorable and sickening if not entirely tragic manner."

"And a nice little windfall for us, Karl," said Lenny. "Always provided that certain people remember to go easy on the incendiaries."

Lenny fired up the fans, and the big SAPS Meat Wagon hovercraft was in the process of hefting itself up on its skirt when the comms unit broke in.

"*Code twenty-three alert from GenTech…*" the SAPS dispatcher said, then rattled off a string of coordinates that would be utterly meaningless to anyone who did not know what a Code Twenty-three meant. Then:

"*All available units required. Do not – repeat, do* not *– engage the primary directly. Standard clean-up and contain, and await suitably qualified assistance…*"

Lenny turned the Meat Wagon in the air, and punched the crash-course coordinates they had received into the autopilot.

"Looks like we'll make the quota after all," he said. "And then some. We're off to Mimsey's World of Adventure."

IN MOST COMMERCIAL processes there is something which might be thought of as the Window of Illusory Desirability – as is well known by anyone who has bought a piece of apparently high-powered computer equipment, at what seems to be an unbelievably knock-down price, only to have the manufacturer roll out a vastly improved version, at a lower price, the very next day (ie anyone who has ever bought a piece of apparently high-powered computer equipment in their lives).

What the Window of Illusory Desirability boils down to, basically, is that when some product or service is becoming obsolescent, there is a window of opportunity when a drastically reduced price will still convince some suckers to buy it.

To take the classic example of buggy-whips: with the supplantation of horse-drawn carriages by the automobile, it's not impossible to imagine the makers of such secondary articles as whips resorting, for a while, to increasingly desperate measures to sell the damn things. Two-for-one offers and the like – which of course resulted in the consumer merely ending up with two completely useless things instead of one.

Of course, the manufacture and selling of whips survives and thrives, now, in certain limited and specialist markets. And the allusion might be seen to be quite apposite in this current case.

During the collapse and consolidation of populations into corporate compound-blocks, the owners of any number of pieces of what had once been prime real-estate realised that what they owned would seen be effectively abandoned and worthless. During that Window of Illusory Desirability, however, they were able to sell off various tracts of land at what appeared to be a bargain price.

Amongst these was a theme park originally the property of a corporation once mighty indeed but long since subsumed into one branch or another of the GenTech Corporation.

In any case, the new owners redressed their acquisition at the minimum of expense – more or less just basically plastering the name *Mimsey* over every occurrence of the name of the previous owners, and tried to rake in as much cash as possible before the world around them finally collapsed.

In this they failed spectacularly, until coming up with a bright if not particularly original idea:

Rather in the same way that whips and so forth had come to change their nature – or at least, had changed the nature of the things they commonly hit – the Mimsey World of Adventure came to cater for a somewhat different market than for which it had first been intended.

The overregulated environments of the compound-blocks had no provision for what might be termed as *adult* entertainment – and only adults, these days, were allowed out into the dangers of the No-Go zone to look for it.

This led an entirely new dimension to the business of dressing people up in costumes.

And certainly to the uses to which animatronic rodents might be put.

FOOTAGE FROM THE swarm of free-floating securicams that blanketed the Mimsey World of Adventure, hooked into the pattern-recognition routines of the security systems – and also, incidentally, gathered material for a wide range of Mimsey brand porno-disks – first showed the intruder as a warped and somewhat bulky but humanoid form blundering in a

kind of shuffling lurch amongst the crowds on Bestiality Avenue.

This did not trigger an alert of any kind because there had been no reports, at this time, of the Mimsey World electro-wire perimeter having been breached. And besides, amongst a crowd of tourists, hookers and other performers variously cosmeticized and costumed, there was nothing inherently out of the ordinary about this figure at all.

Security tracking-systems picked this figure up again, with the first overt overtones of suspicion, in Panchakamara Street, in the shadow of the Wheel of Frottage, overturning a dog-burger stand, swatting the canine-costumed proprietor out of the way and attempting to gorge itself on the uncooked meat extruding from the patty-ejection tanks.

This, apparently, was not to the figure's taste. It projectile vomited with such force as to knock several bystanders from their feet, then ran into the crowd – security tracking-systems now following it with some quite actual degree of alarm.

It might be noted that the creature did not seriously hurt anyone, in its erratic path through the Mimsey World crowds, until it reached the Grotto of Sanguinary Delights.

Possibly the nature and scent of the fluids involved here maddened it. Far more probably, it is because Mimsey World security staff had by now at last caught up with it, and at this point one attempted to take it down with a taser-discharge.

In any event, it was at this point the creature – now unquestionably a *creature* rather than a human figure of any kind – transformed in a blaze of light so bright that it knocked out several of the recording microcams. Those that survived, on the periphery of the blast, reported images of a shifting, hulking mass. There were vague suggestions of writhing tentacles, and far more definite suggestions of teeth and claws.

No two microcam reports – and certainly no two human reports, from those humans on the ground who remained alive – quite agreed as to the creature's ultimate form. There seemed to be some aspect to its very shape in the world that rendered on areas of the human visual cortex as simply null.

Security-tracking now reported the creature pelting from the Grotto of Sanguinary Delights in a blur of speed almost impossible for the unassisted human eye to catch. While the crowds exploded apart, quite literally, at its passage, it was possible that there was no actively vicious intent, and that the creature was merely attempting to find some means of escape.

If this was so, it was particularly unfortunate that the path of intended escape lead directly to the House of Autoerotic Strangulation, one of the Mimsey World's most popular and crowded attractions.

And from this point on the carnage had to be seen to be believed.

And you can see it now for only $79.99, on *When Vacations Go Bad: Extreme*. Press your red interactive button now.

LENNY AND KARL, the SAPS paramedics, had truly died and gone to heaven. Phrases involving the words *happy*, *pigs* and *shit* came to mind – though it was probably more akin to a pair of vampires after an explosion in a slaughterhouse.

They had landed their Meat Wagon on the scene to find a number of SAPS units already there, but that didn't matter. There were enough pickings for everybody. Forget about making the quota – they were well into bonuses and overtime here.

Frantic happy minutes were spent filling up their storage units to capacity. They didn't even need to fill the cracks with limbs or other organs.

Market conditions, at the moment, were for some reason placing a premium on human heads – and there were more than enough of these available without so much as looking at the other small-time stuff twice.

Possibly they had become a little delirious, high on the fact of this totally unexpected and lucrative windfall, but when Karl had suggested checking out the House of Autoerotic Strangulation, Lenny had not argued too much.

"Code twenty-three," Karl had said. "That means a Classified Test Subject on the loose from one of the Big Guys. I

never seen anything like that. I bet it'd be a fuckin' sight to see."

"Yeah, right, Karl," Lenny had said. "If we lived long enough to fuckin' *tell* about it."

"We won't get close or anything," Karl had assured him. "Close enough to get a look and then we just duck the fuck out."

He became thoughtful.

"You never know, though. Maybe it's filled up on whatever it eats. Maybe we could get a chance to pull it down ourselves. I can think of lots the Big Guys could do for two guys who manage to pull it down."

At the time it had seemed, if not a plan, then at least something worth checking out just to see if it might be possible. Now, in the reeking chamber that had once been the House of Strangulation, Lenny just didn't think so.

Lenny's working life didn't lend itself much to squeamishness, but the current circumstances were definitely heading into the country of the too much.

Possibly it was all the evidence of what the hanging bodies, those who had not managed to join the mass exodus on the arrival of the Code 23, had been about before they died.

The basic purpose of the chamber had precluded bright lighting in the first place; now even the blacklights were out. In the foetid darkness, Lenny half-expected to hear the rasp and rumble of some Great Beast's breath.

He'd have preferred that to the clink of chains in what was otherwise silence, come to think of it. At least that might give some clue as to what was lurking in the dark, and where.

He realised that he lad lost contact with Karl.

"Karl?" he rasped, casting about with his SAP-issue flashlight. Flashes of variously depending bodies catching the beam. Nothing more.

Then, off to one side – and literally in the space of half a second – the sound of something scything through flesh, the *clunch-clunch-clunch* of impossibly busy mastication, and then dead silence again.

Whatever had just happened, had happened too fast for Lenny's mind to process.

"Karl?" he called again, still casting somewhat bemusedly around with the flashlight.

Something bony and razor-sharp swung in out of the darkness. Before it lopped his head clean off, Lenny caught the impression that it seemed to be attached to a tube of fleshy and possibly living matter.

Lenny's body spasmed and keeled over, the head spinning off into the dark, to rebound off a chain and fetch up wedged against one of the hanging bodies in a manner that would have almost certainly startled the owner of it, had they been alive.

All of this had happened so suddenly, though, that it was some time before the impulses in his brain shut completely down. Thus, with the last of his dying perceptions, he was able to perceive the sudden flash of alien light from nearby, the subsonic-loaded roar of something in pain and the thump of something big hitting the ground.

He was able to hear the cheerful, female voice saying: "You see what I mean, Masterton? I told you it was a good idea to arrange things so some of the dumb SAPs went in first.'

11.

… AND WE'RE OUTSIDE *(I don't know how we got here), shot from the geodesics to the gravepits, and she's leading me, sylph-like now, albified. She's shucking non-essentials left and centre as she hauls me through the mud and ruptured coffins, past the thieves new-gutted hanging from their ropes; past the shamen with their mortified and wormy hearts. The schimiraras an th' tomajawks an knifs with grey hairs stick to the heft. She's positively glowing.*

You made this, she's telling me. Do you see? You made it and you own it and it's yours.

I slipped on something (momentarily). Ointment made from monkshood, nightshade, hemlock blended with the fat of children. They use it, apparently, to fly.

She dips a wafer in the stringy half-clotted mess (it's something else, now, and something not entirely pleasant) and proffers it (I'm kneeling, now, before her; begging for something that I cannot now recall). The monkey still hanging from my neck, enraged, attempts to snatch it away.

She avoids the little clutching hands. Looks down on me. You really don't, she says. You have no idea. You made yourself forget.

Her fingers taste of earth and shit and chemicals as she shoves them into my mouth, and works it open, and at last administers the eight-pointed communion wafer.

* * *

"THE PROCESS OF living," said Masterton with relaxed and somewhat weaselly smugness, "is one of dynamic recursion. We do all this crap, all manner of crap, and like as not it comes to nothing and we just end up back where we started."

Eddie Kalish scowled around himself at the Factory medical-centre room.

Everything was as he had left it, save that Laura Palmer's blood had been cleaned from the wall – and for the flexible yet stout woven polycarbon straps, around his forearms and shins, that now secured him to the frame of the bed.

"Screw you," he said. Whatever the Zarathustra processes had done for him, in this form at least, they hadn't made him strong enough to break loose from woven polycarbon straps.

"And the wit just keeps on scintillating," Masterton said, still with that same shit-eating grin.

"Imagine it as similar to the processes of any other life, if it makes you at all happier," he continued. People wake up, they do stuff and then they go to sleep again. Wake up, do stuff and go to sleep all over again. We just run through the iterations over and over again, with minor variations, until we get to the point where we're doing things more-or-less right. Like that computer program about an ant, or whatever it is, that blunders around erratically for a while and then starts progressing on a line.

"Now, are you finally going to stop thrashing around and screaming abuse and injuring yourself long enough so I can give you the true skinny? It really won't take that long, and at the moment you're just wasting everybody's time, including your own."

Eddie considered this. When he had first woken up – again – here in the Factory an indeterminate number of days before, the knowledge of his recapture, together with disjointed half-memories of what he had done in the interim, had alternately plunged him into hysteria and catatonic shock. The latter, of course, being exacerbated by an increased regimen of anaes-thetic hypos.

Things had not exactly been improved by the fact that Mas-terton had insisted on showing him, in more lucid moments,

securicam footage of the events that had occurred out in the No-Go and the Mimsey World of Adventure.

The thing that Eddie Kalish had turned into. The things that he had done.

Now it seemed that, temporarily at least, the sheer hysteria had burned itself out. It was time to start thinking again. Time to think in terms of formulating a plan. And for that Eddie needed hard information.

"So why don't you tell me all about it?" he said. "Pretty please, with sugar and shit on top?"

"Screw you," said Masterton, without apparent rancour. "First thing I gotta tell you – which you probably worked out yourself already – as that as a part of the Zarathustra process we've been electromagnetically pulse-pumping data into your head. Uploading you with all manner of useful info, including an enhanced vocabulary – and hard though it is to imagine, it's pretty much working. What's a *Benedicta?*"

"An angel-girl," said Eddie, automatically. "The sort of girl who, when you see her for the first time, she's like some evidence of God. Baudelaire wrote a prose poem about it–"

"And there you go," said Masterton. "You didn't get it right, but it was a reasonable guess, and a while back you couldn't read the caption under a *Hustler* cartoon without moving your lips. And I'll bet you dollars to day-old dogshit you never even heard of Baudelaire."

Eddie thought about it. "What good does me knowing about Baudelaire do?"

"'Cause we're turning you into a fag, all right?" Masterton shrugged. "It doesn't have to mean anything, and a lot of it's just random. The more you know, the more you have to think *with*, you know? Bang it around into new shapes in your head.

"Anyhoo. The process messes with your dream-imagery as the brain tries to sort it all out – but you'll have noticed how your dreams are getting *seriously* out of whack, you know what I mean?"

Masterton moved around the bed forcing Eddie to strain his neck to keep him in sight.

"If you sat down and tried," Masterton continued, "knowing all the stuff that we're streaming you, knowing the stuff that happened in your life, there's still shit coming in from somewhere entirely *else*. Information there's no possible way you should know. Some whole other world.

"That's because you're part of an experimental project, classified on absolutely the highest level. The people you killed in the sex-park, they'd be dead anyway now if you hadn't killed them. As are maybe a couple of hundred who caught direct sight of you and survived."

The enormity of this took some little while to sink in to Eddie. "How can you…" he managed at last.

"We threw in a lot of wet-team resources and didn't care if it got messy," said Masterton, artfully failing to get the point. "You know, in an extremely prejudicial sort of way. We doctored the microcam-evidence, too, to remove anything distinctive or identifiable about you, even in your transformed state. Any detail that might possibly trace you back to us.

"And speaking of which: the point of the programme, so far as you and your dreams are concerned, is that we've added a certain… extra little something to your Zarathustra mix. From a whole other source. And it's to do with the way the world's been getting weird these last few decades."

"You don't have to tell me about the world getting weird," said Eddie, more or less for the sake of something to say.

"Oh, I don't mean just the low-grade madness you'd have encountered back in Cracker Ridge, New Mexico, or wherever the hell it was," said Masterton. "There's stuff happening out there now that makes the shit that happened to Des Moines look sick.

"The big flip-over happened sometime around the turn of the millennium – I mean, before that, you could take a through-line through history and with a bit of work, and rather like dreams, you could see how it all sorta fit together and *worked* even if only with hindsight.

"That just doesn't fly any more, on anything other than a limited and local basis. Things are becoming discontinuous –

like the informational Singularity they predicted we'd be living in as far back as 1972, but bleeding into the physical and actual level. Reality-glitches, temporal-perception-glitches, mass-hallucinations." Masterton sighed. "Ask anybody who knows, they'll give you a different take. A different explanation for it. Contact with alien entities, or extradimensional entities, has disrupted the world on a fundamental level – or human perceptions of it, which pretty much amounts to the same thing so far as humans are concerned."

Masterton moved back around to the other side of the bed. Eddie gave up on trying to keep him in sight and stared at the ceiling instead.

"Or maybe we're seeing the first evidence of time-travel, the first wave of contact from the future impacting on the timeline. A bunch of the more fundamentalist whackos are convinced that we're just living in the Last Days, with the Maw of Hell opening up and demons coming through to clear the way for the Great Beast…"

"So what's your theory?" Eddie asked.

"What?" said Masterton.

"What do *you* think is really happening to the world? You know, personally."

"Well, you know, personally I think it's to do with four-dimensional space," said Masterton. A little defensively, Eddie thought. "The three-dimensional construct we perceive of as Space is falling through the fourth dimension of Time – that's why travelling through time doesn't take any actual *effort*, yeah? Thing is, we're not just travelling through time at a second-per-second, we're *accelerating* at a second-per-second-*per*-second.

"Things are speeding up as we come closer to whatever temporally-gravitational source we're falling towards and we splash like a watermelon thrown off a compound-block. The cracks are beginning to show. Or maybe we've smacked into something on the way down…"

Masterton visibly took control of himself, then shrugged.

"I have to admit that I haven't quite worked it all out yet," he said. "I was, like, totally stoned when I thought of it. I also

thought, for a while, that the three-dimensional construct that we know as the world, seen from outside, was bright purple and shaped like a walrus."

Eddie Kalish nodded, understandingly. It seemed like the only way, at this point, that someone would eventually get around to loosening the polycarbon straps.

"Anyhoo," said Masterton. "The primary cause doesn't matter, any more than you need a thorough grounding in atomic theory to know that if you bang a couple of pounds of enriched plutonium together you get one big bang.

"The plain fact is that cracks are appearing in the world, allowing the incursion of elements from some other reality, like the way you sometimes get references and ideas from somewhere entirely else dropped into a book.

"What we're trying to do, here in the Factory, is to patch elements of that new… call it *subtext*… into the existing structural coding of the Zarathustra lexicon. We call the end result the Loup."

"The Loup?" said Eddie, completely failing to get it.

"Ell-oh-you-pee," said Masterton. "Scots for *leap*, apparently. Quantum jumps and so forth. Plus it's French for *wolf* – bringing in the whole idea of lycanthropy. For obvious reasons."

Half-buried memories of the carnage in the Mimsey San Angeles Adventure surfaced with a vengeance. Eddie gulped and shuddered as he tried to force them down. He strained his neck again to face Masterton.

"What happened out there?" he asked, when he could more or less speak again. "What did I turn into?"

"Near as we can tell," said Masterton, "the Loup opens up a… portal, let's call it, and *something* comes through. The precise nature of it is still unclear. It doesn't seem to think in what we imagine of as human terms, though it certainly has impulses and reactions.

"The Loup converts energy from the life-forms around it, seemingly at random, and uses it to transform the host. We think it's trying to build the equivalent of a pressure-suit, so it can survive in this world…"

Eddie Kalish was following all of this. It was just that he couldn't believe it.

"Why the hell would you *do* this to me?" he said at last.

Masterton frowned. "I told you, you're nothing. You just happened to be on hand."

"No, I mean why would you do it to *anybody*? What possible use would it be?"

"It's useful if it's contained and controlled," said Masterton. "Trix Desoto was the first test subject who developed techniques for controlling it. You wouldn't believe some of the things that girl can do."

Abruptly, his expression clouded into one of bad-tempered spite.

"But there's no point telling you now," he continued. "We were gonna stream those hard-earned control-techniques to you, on the subconscious level, but you went off the damn script and bugged out. Now you're going to have to learn them the hard way – if you end up learning them at all. Look familiar?"

Masterton, Eddie saw, was holding up a hypo of the sort with which Eddie was being periodically tranqued.

"This contains a compound we call the Leash," said Masterton. "And don't even bother to try working out what that means. The name describes what it does, not what's in it or how it works.

"It keeps the thing inside you dormant. You go twelve hours without a booster-shot and the thing goes overt. Then it tears everything it can get its claws on apart, which is sort of an inconvenience for anything it gets its claws on. And plus it gives out a psychic trace like you wouldn't believe.

"We don't get there in time to haul it back, it tears itself apart under its own internal forces – which is certainly going to be an inconvenience for *you*..."

"I seem to recall," said Eddie, "you've already told me you own my ass. So what difference does all this make?"

"Just emphasising the point," said Masterton. "I let you loose, you're still on a choke-chain. There's a reason why we're

inoculating people with the Loup, a specific job we need them to do.

"Haulage and delivery to… well, let's just say that where you're going, where you're going to end up, only someone infected by the Loup has any chance of surviving.

"At the moment, apart from Trix Desoto, you're the nearest thing we have to a viable option. And time's getting tight."

12.

ON HIS ATTEMPT at escaping the Factory, Eddie Kalish had not bothered to check out the contents of the warehouse-space around it. On the whole, he realised, it was fortunate that he had not.

Had he stuck so much as his head through the doors, without clearance, then that head would have been burnt off by the plasma-ejectors of automated defences – whether the powers that be had wanted him kept alive and intact or not.

Now, in the company of Trix Desoto, he wandered through the big steel caverns. He somehow expected his footsteps to echo off the walls, for all that sound was as deadened in here as in any recording studio.

The inner walls of the warehouses crawled with polyceramic baffles and steel mesh designed to disrupt tracksat scanning that could ordinarily see right through the flat surfaces of buildings.

Possibly the hybrid processes of the Loup really had left him smarter, because something occurred to him that he was sure never would have, in what he was increasingly coming to think of as his previous life.

"Doesn't that look suspicious in itself?" he asked. "You know, a NeoGen tracksat looks down and sees a bunch of totally disrupted forms?"

Trix Desoto snorted.

"Give us some credit," she said. "The baffles are constructed to give the impression of old packing cases and the occasional scurrying rat."

Indeed, looking up, Eddie could see a lump of vaguely rat-shaped thermal biogel being moved around by a clockwork-driven arm. The use of clockwork, presumably, prevented the mechanism from being identified as such.

It all seemed a bit Rube Goldberg to Eddie. If he could only work out what a *Rube Goldberg* was...

Most of the space under the baffles was taken up with the big hulks of Behemoth rigs, of a similar sort to those Eddie had seen when he had first encountered Trix.

As had been the case then, the tanker-like construction of most of them was simply camouflage. For all that they were plastered with Hazmat decals, suggesting that a breach would release the kind of chemical-waste sludge that would seriously bring down anybody's day, the hatches were open to reveal simple compartment space.

Workers in sterile med-tech coveralls were busily filling the compartments with what appeared to be thermos canisters. There were thousands of these canisters. There was no indication as to what they might contain... but the size and squat proportions of them left Eddie decidedly uneasy.

"Couple of hours before they finish loading the Brain Train," said Trix Desoto, instantly confirming Eddie's unease.

"And what are we calling the Behemoths themselves?" asked Eddie. "Think Tankers?"

Trix Desoto snorted again, this time it seemed with suppressed laughter rather than contempt.

This little instant of human contact left Eddie feeling momentarily weird. He didn't know what to think about it.

"So how did *you* get roped into all this..?" he ventured at last.

"None of your damn business," Trix Desoto said, flatly. It was like a shutter coming down. "I might tell you the story of my life, someday, but it won't be today. For the moment you can just keep your grubby fingers out of my head."

"Suit yourself," said Eddie Kalish.

Off to one side of the warehouse, a bunch of outriders in bulky leather-skinned body armour were checking the gyro-systems on their flywheel-driven motorsickles. A small group of them were doing the traditional thing of sharing a smoke directly under the sign on the wall that told them, in huge letters, not to do that very thing.

Eddie glanced from them back to Trix, in her skin-tight patent leather, and raised an eyebrow. "You're gonna be coming it like the biker chick for this thing, yes?"

"I'm going to be riding in command-and-control this time out," Trix said, her manner easing up again, just a little, now the conversation had returned to the job at hand. "Doing the Third Assistant to the Attaché thing, you know? Anyone from the outside looking in, I'm a console-jockey. From the inside out I'm in Command."

"Good for you," said Eddie. "So where do I fit into your whole command-structure thing?"

"For the moment, till we get where we're going, you're a semi-autonomous unit. You're gonna be running vanguard; our eyes and ears in front."

"And when we get there, wherever it is?" Eddie asked, uneasily recalling what Masterton had said about only he and Trix being the only two who carried a viable strain of the Loup.

"That's need-to-know," said Trix Desoto. "And you don't need to, yet. For now, your function is to help the Brain Train get through in the first place, and you should concentrate on that."

Eddie concentrated on it – or at least, he thought about it.

"Front-runner just seems like one hell of a responsibility, is all," he said. "I mean, you can pump my head full of all the new info and vocabulary you like; the fact remains that I've never

done anything like it before. I just don't have the experience. It's a screw-up waiting to happen, is all I'm saying."

"You've got experience," said Trix Desoto. "You spent years out on the roads and you survived."

"I spent years dicking around, never going anywhere much and rabbiting at the first scent of danger," Eddie said.

"Yeah, well, those are the senses and instincts the front-runner needs," said Trix. "Your job is to sense the danger, then rat out and cover your ass while the heavy-duty guys deal with the actual combat. I reckon we can trust to the Leash that you won't rat out too far."

Eddie nodded, feeling depressed. Trix would, of course, be supplying him with his twelve-hourly dose of the Leash for the duration of the run.

Come what may, the life of one Eddie Kalish would be inextricably linked to the fortunes of the Brain Train.

"Besides," said Trix, "you're really not going to be doing much more, in the end, than sit there on your ass. You're going to have help."

"IF IT ISN'T a personal thing about the story of your life," said Eddie, "what do you think of this thing about cracks in the world and stuff? The thing about how the Loup is supposed to actually work?"

They were working their way through the loading-activity around the Behemoths towards a partitioned-off area before the main doors of the warehouse.

Eddie had noted this when coming in, and had wondered what the partitions concealed. Only he hadn't wondered enough to take a look, on account of the fact that a security-system plasma ejector had started tracking him, with a *whirr* of servos, when he had gotten too close.

"What?" said Trix, who seemed a little lost in her own thoughts. "Why do you ask?"

"Well, it just sounded like bullshit, you know? The sort of shit you dream up when you've been dancing with Mr Brownstone. But Masterton said that everyone has their own

idea of what's really going on, so I just wanted to hear what you think is really happening, is all."

"I don't think about it, much," said Trix. "To the extent I do, I think it's just another way that the world's a sex-killer."

"What?" said Eddie. "I mean, a what?"

"Sex-killer. Whoever you are, the world just screws you. It screws you up and screws you over, and when it's had enough of screwing you it kills you. Simple as that. Last few years, it's just stopped dicking around and decided to be up front about it."

As a general philosophy of life, there was much in it that Eddie could get right behind. Something inside him, however, was saying that it was all too pat in its bleakness and resignation – and that some large part of Trix Desoto didn't believe a word of it herself.

Just another front.

"So if that's just what the world is," he said, "if that's all there is, why even bother to keep living?"

"What's the alternative?" asked Trix. "Here we go."

They had reached the partitioned–off area, and Trix slid one of the partitions back to reveal what – for one Eddie Kalish at least – was a reason to keep on living at least for a while.

"There's your help," said Trix Desoto.

The red skin of the Testostorossa gleamed in the pristine, liquid way that spoke of either fresh wet paint or a well-nigh impervious monomolecular shell. Eddie Kalish had lived around vehicles for most of his life, in any number of states of repair. He had thought he knew from vehicles of any kind.

He had never known an automobile, in and of itself, could be so beautiful. Wonderingly, disbelievingly, he reached out a hand to stroke the liquid-seeming shell.

Smoothly, ramping on an exponential curve, the engine came to life. There was a kind of throaty roar to it, which Eddie would later learn to be due to integral booster-units – the hydrofusion equivalent of turbo-charging.

"*Get your fuckin' hand off me,*" the Testostorossa growled, in the voice of a New York cabbie. "*You a fuckin' fag or what?*"

* * *

THE DOORS OF the warehouse rolled up, and the security-system plasma ejectors racked themselves back on their servos.

The front-runner sped out like a red streak, hi-impact suspension taking care of the worst of what had might once been a street but was not little more than a debris-strewn track.

It put some distance between itself and the warehouse complex, then slowed to match that of the Brain Train tankers which were now emerging, the motorsickle outriders fanning out to bracket them to far as was possible in the current urban conditions.

Over to one side, in the wreckscape of the No-Go there was the rattle of automatic fire, the flash and smoke of frag-detonations. This was a common occurrence at the beginning of any transport-operation: each of the various multicorps had arrangements with one or another of the various tribes that infested the No-Go. NeoGen, or MegaStel, or any number of other concerns, bribed guys to disrupt GenTech traffic as a matter of principle – and GenTech had guys on the ground to take out any source of disruption.

The Brain Train convoy headed up on the somewhat tortuous route that would take it northwards through the San Angeles Sprawl and at last onto the pristine blacktop of the Interways… and an entirely other kind and degree of danger.

The sheer size of the operation made any attempt to run covertly not even worth thinking about. Lights blazing, loaded up for mutant bear, the Brain Train was a sight to see.

MASTERTON WASN'T WATCHING it. He wasn't even tracking the Brain Train's progress via the tracksat readouts in the Factory communications suite. All the same, he knew precisely where it was.

"*Sama slektli,*" he was saying, prostrate before his totems in the spare and austere cell that served as his working space and living space combined. "*Tara oorsi sa mamda lami se tarakogla me so sani ta deloka de somata so se hakara de sao soma…*"

The words, had there been anyone here to listen to them, would have struck this nonexistent listener as pure nonsense,

without basis in any known human language-structure, even to the point of having the glossolaic quality of speaking in tongues.

Indeed, that was rather the point.

Likewise, the collection of artefacts and totems on the floor before him appeared to have no real sense of significance: nothing but a random collection of garbage and junk, the detailing of which would serve no actual or useful purpose.

And, again, this was the point.

The words and totems had, in fact, no more significance than the static and distortion coming from a radio receiver when hunting between stations — save that, at some specific point on the dial, one can learn to recognise a particular blend and texture in the static, and know that one is coming close to whatever station one is actually searching for.

The words and totems merely directed the mind towards… a *place* for which there are no ordinary terms of human reference.

Masterton looked up.

The air before him shimmered as though with heat-haze — then split open as cleanly and neatly as a razor slits a polythene sheet. A matched pair of barbs, each trailing a thing fleshy line, shot from the slit and speared Masterton, punching through his shades and burying themselves deep into the eye sockets beneath.

The lines connecting Masterton to the rip in the fabric of the world twitched and pulsed; some kind of exchange was taking place. Masterton drooled.

"*Salekmi tekla,*" he said through his slack mouth. "*Samo de talekli sama*… Food for you," he continued in more or less distinguishable tones, as though some synchronisation had been reached with whatever it was behind the slit in the world. "Sending food for you. Food for you now. Food for your mouth."

reprise:
reset settings
to start

THE SEVERCY SISTERS hit them as they went through Checkpoint 9.

The gangcult had been stalking them for maybe ten miles, now, segueing in on one or other of the outriders to have an exploratory crack then peeling off, weighing up the defence-response. Now the core mass of them piled it on, coming in from both sides.

"The Sisters are small fry," Eddie Kalish said, quick-scanning the pattern-recognition specs and stats streaming across his Testostorossa's HUD. "They're just little girls with a grudge. No real kill power to speak. They don't care about the Brain Train – they're just coming in pincer-wise to knock off the front-runner."

"*Yeah, well,*" the Testostorossa said, diodes rippling on its voice-display, "*that would be us. What's the matter, faggot? Too much of a queer to wanna fuck some girlies?*"

"I just think it's a waste." Inwardly some large part of Eddie groaned. He didn't mean any of this macho bullshit, but the Testostorossa was getting to him. He was starting to get the idea that killing people with an asinine quip on your lips was just flat-out murder.

Through the shotgun window a girl in torn leather and spikes leant from her quad-bike and swung what appeared to be an exact copy of a medieval morningstar. It looked pretty lethal, but the business end of it rebounded from the monatomic carbon shell of the Testostorossa to no effect whatsoever.

The Sister snarled in pique. She couldn't have been more than sixteen years old.

"Anyhow," Eddie said, "These kids just aren't tooled-up enough to hurt us."

"*Yeah, but they're drawing attention to us,*" the Testostorossa said. "*Lots of other fuckers out there, waiting to sit up and take notice – and they're packing enough heavy stuff to make us go bang-splat.*"

Seemingly of their own accord, multidirectional scatterguns extended, locked and loaded.

"*I'm scraping these bitches off us as of now,*" the Testostorossa said. "*You just keep that pinhead of yours on driving me.*"

Eddie gunned the turbo-acceleration and sighed. How the hell had he ever gotten himself into this..?

third quadrant: impactor road

FROM A BEDROOM a roscoe said: "Whr-r-rang!" and a lead pill split the ozone past my noggin… Kane Frewster was on the floor. There was a bullet-hole through his think-tank. He was as dead as a fried oyster.

"Dark Star of Death"
Spicy Detective
January 1938

supplementary data: a common childhood

THE LIGHT FELL in actinic, dust-laden shafts through holes eaten in the rusting corrugated sides of the shed; inched across the ragged forms huddled on the dirt floor. A number of rats slunk through the hut, with a silent inconspicuousness and an utter lack of scurrying that might have seemed, to some observer, slightly overplayed and unnatural. Something the rats had learnt consciously rather than by instinct.

This demeanour had developed in response to the fact that should a rat be detected, here and now, it would last about as long as it took to be torn apart and the pieces squabbled over and eaten. Such useful protein-supplements were beyond price – if anyone had even had sufficient resources to know what a price was – here in the camp.

The gentle purr of an engine outside. A rat which had been, very quietly, very surreptitiously, investigating a particular huddled bundle of rags on the grounds that it might just have stopped moving for good, now joined its fellows in streaking for a bolt-hole in the side of the shed – a trajectory so complicated, designed so that it escaped the slightest breath of detection, as to be barely physically possible.

The bundle that the rat had been perusing twitched, then stirred, then uncurled from the foetal form in which it had slept to show a pinched, pale face. A girl of maybe twelve years old, possibly slightly older, but her state of chronic malnutrition made it difficult to tell. Her matted, filth-encrusted hair could have been any colour. One eye was filmed by a cataract, which glistened silver-grey in the dim light. There was a large, open sore on the side of her neck.

Rubbing absently at the sore, the girl picked her way, silently and cautiously as any rat, through the other occupants of the shed. Heading for the door, even though it would of course still be barred from the outside. She intended to be amongst the first into the food-crush, this morning; she needed to conserve her strength. The last thing she needed at this point was a fight.

Dimly, she recalled a time when she'd had milk-teeth, friable as chalk due to lack of calcium in her diet, but they had at least served to give her some minute edge as a weapon. Her adult teeth, however, had simply never begun to grow. She didn't even know that she was supposed to have them.

Outside, the sound of engines acquired extra harmonics as they were joined by the tones of another. The girl had never heard that particular sound before, and curiosity got the best of her. She stuck her good eye to a rust-hole eaten in the wall and looked out into the Camp.

Big yellow half-track carriers were parked in the compound. There were little blue bubbles on the top of their cabs, two to a cab, in which small, illuminated, reflective saucers revolved so that it looked as if the little blue bubbles were flashing with light. The girl didn't know what the vehicles were, of course; her only experience with vehicles was the slop-truck that delivered what passed for food and removed waste. She wondered, vaguely, what the people of the Camp were going to be fed today. With trucks so big and splendid as that, it must be something very special indeed.

Off to one side, she caught a glimpse of men in coveralls busily setting up what looked like a monkey-puzzle of steel,

fluorescent tubes and medical equipment. Other men, in bulky yellow corslets of polycarbon body-armour, looked on, hefting black objects that looked a little like the shock-sticks used by the Camp guards, but bigger. The girl wondered what those things were – just not so much that she wanted to be the one who found out.

Behind her, the other occupants of the shed were stirring awake. The girl found herself in something of a quandary. Something new was happening, and it could either be something good or bad. No way of telling which.

Deciding that it was probably better to be more circumspect, the girl backed off from the door and returned to the main crush of occupants, not so far that she would end up at the back. If something bad was going to happen then it could happen to somebody else first. If something good, then there was a chance there'd still be some left when it got to her.

SOME HALF AN hour later, the yellow-corsleted men unbarred the door of the shed and herded the occupants out, blinking in the sudden sunlight, into the compound.

Now the girl stood towards one side of a line of children, their ages ranging from those of toddler to adolescent. From this vantage point she could see what was happening to several of the sheds that made up the Camp.

Men in coveralls, with masks over their heads, had opened up the metal boxes sunk into the sides of these sheds – the boxes that the girl, and for that matter anyone else in the Camp, had attempted to get into at some time or another, and see what was inside, purely for the sake of something to do – and were loading them with pressurised canisters. One of them tested a canister as the girl watched, twisting a tap on its neck, then nodded.

Another pair of men were wandering between the rows of standing children. One held a portable data-terminal, the other a camera – though the girl of course did not know what either of those things was.

They stopped in front of the girl.

"You're a little sweetheart, aren't you?" he said. "Isn't she a little sweetheart, Karl?"

"She's a sweetheart, Lenny," said Karl. "Yes indeedy."

"Give us a smile, sweetheart," said Lenny, sticking the camera in her face.

The girl smiled.

"Turn your head, sweetheart," said Karl.

She turned her head.

"Visually, Karl, she could be good," said Lenny, studying the display on his data terminal. "Don't worry about the rickets or the incipient lupus, those are correctable. She's got the general facial-structure, that's what counts. Pity about that sore, though. Looks viral to me. She's gonna need reconstruction, and that means, maybe, more bucks upfront than GenTech Entertainment needs."

Karl shrugged. "So, we take a flier, Lenny, and if it doesn't work out then GenTech Entertainment shoots her in profile. People won't be looking at her neck, much, anyway. 'Cept the ones who are into it. There are those. Say something, sweetheart."

This last to the girl, who dredged up as much basic English as she knew how to speak. It wasn't so much that she was following orders as that it cost her nothing to do so, it was something to do, and she might as well do it as not.

"What do you want me to say?" she asked.

"I like the voice," said Karl. "Personality."

"Microtremors show an incredible potential range," said Lenny, waggling his data unit meaningfully. "I think we might just have ourselves a screamer here."

"What's your name, sweetheart?" asked Karl.

"Trix," the girl said. "My name's Trix."

Nice name," said Karl. "Very apt." He pulled a paint-stick from his pocket and scrawled a small collection of symbols down her arm. "Now what I want you to do, sweetheart, is go over there. They'll take care of you over there."

He shoved her off in the direction of the biomedical monkey-puzzle, and big, old people in white who would babble about

path-testing and debriding, and shove a needle in her, arm and that was the last thing she remembered for a while.

HER EYES AND lips were crusted with dried mucus when she woke, at last, to find herself lying on something flat, and impossibly soft, and with an IV-drip in her arm.

Dark shapes hazed before her against a blazing white light. Something hard and shockingly cold was pressed against the sore in the side of her neck, and she tried to jerk her head away. She found that her cheeks, hoever, were pressed between two padded blocks, rendering her head immobile.

Something she simply did not recognise was water, for the simple reason that it was not sludgy and stinking, dropped onto her eyes and lips. She opened her eyes.

A man with a shaven head and a jet-black Suit loomed over her. Impossibly old, even older than the guards in the Camp. Possibly even thirty, if such a thing could be imagined.

Something cold and slim and tubular slid into her mouth. She tried to spit it out.

The man slapped her. Not particularly hard, just hard enough to hurt.

"Drink it," he said.

Trix drank what she would later learn to be fruit juice warmed to body-heat so that the basic unfamiliarity of it would not be rejected by her body. All the same, her blood-sugar rocketed too fast for an atrophied liver to even begin to cope – and due to the clamped position of her head, she almost choked to death before hands, off to one side that she couldn't see, found an aspirator.

After she was more or less settled, the man looked down at her and smiled. It was probably meant to be reassuring, but even Trix could see that it was just a movement of his mouth; he'd trained his mouth to move in a certain precise way and didn't mean it at all. Even though she couldn't see them for the obloids of black glass that covered them, Trix knew that the smile never had and never would touch his eyes.

"Sorry about that," the man said. "We'll have to dilute that for a while. At least until we bulk you up a bit with glucotics." He paused, looking at her thoughtfully. "Do you know, you really are a lucky little girl indeed."

Trix just looked up at him. She didn't feel particularly lucky. Then again, she didn't have all that much to compare "luck" to.

"You're a very lucky girl indeed because we've been looking out for you. We here at GenTech. Looking out for people just like you."

The man did the thing with his mouth again.

"You can call me Masterton," he said. "We're going to do great things. Would I lie to you?'

13.

UP THROUGH PASADENA *and then they hit the Glendale Blockade. Eddie hauled the Testostorossa back and let a modified Behemoth, the front end reinforced and fitted with hydraulic rams, take them through under main force.*

The good citizens of Glendale scattered and the barrier went to pieces; the Brain Train made it through encountering nothing heavier than disorganised small-arms fire.

That gave the Brain Train a straight run west to San Fernando, before hitting what had once been Route 14 and turning north.

"I FEEL LIKE some music," Eddie Kalish told the Testostorossa. "Switch on the radio and find some tunes."

"What, are your hands tired?" the Testostorossa asked him with heavy sarcasm. *"You poor thing. All that beating off guys' cocks, I'll bet. Fuckin' do it yourself."*

Eddie was wishing that whoever had programmed the Testerossa's AI had gone a little easier on the virtual personality. Or given it a completely different one, come to that. The relatively limited amount of processing power that a car, supercharged or not, was able to lug around led to semi-sentient entities with decidedly one-track character traits.

He was also, absolutely, not going to admit that while he had received a thorough grounding in the Testostorossa's systems and controls by way of the Loup – in much the same way as it had allowed him to operate the data-systems back in the Factory – this had for some reason not extended to an ability to operate the built-in entertainment set.

The fact was, with a large proportion of the US population turning to a life on the move, the number of radio stations competing for bandwidth had skyrocketed. It took insanely complicated receiver-controls to pull anything at all out of this jumble of signals in the first place, let alone something which one might enjoy listening to.

The radio receiver crawled with knobs and dials, and Eddie didn't have the first clue as to where to start.

"Just do it, okay?" he said. "It comes down to it, and it doesn't go against the Mission Directives Masterton loaded you up with, you have to do what I say. So I'm fucking *ordering* you, okay? And if you dare put out 'It's Raining Men', 'Boystown' or anything at all by the goddamn Village People, I shall personally open up your hood with a can-opener and see what your artificial brains look like after being fucked over with a monkey wrench. Are we clear?"

"*Suit your fucking self*," said the Testostorossa. It squeal-blipped through the stations, most of which seemed to be playing the latest track by somebody called Freak-E and of whom Eddie had never heard, and settled finally on something with a pair of interminably duelling banjos.

Eddie decided that no music at all would be better than that, found the power switch and shut the radio off.

"What's the matter," said the Testostorossa. "Didn't like it? Seems to me, you'd be a fan of Country with a big C. Something with a big C, anywise."

UP AROUND MOJAVE, they ran into a gangcult calling themselves the Long Reds – not, the Testostorossa's HUD explained rather snottily, on its targeting profile, because of any perceived kinship with American Indians, but because of the long red stains they commonly left their victims in on the blacktop.

Eddie streamed the targeting data back to Trix in the Brain Train Command rig, then bugged out. Dodged through the Long Red horde with AI-assisted efficiency and put in some distance.

Some few minutes later, Trix Desoto broke in on the comsat link: "*Get your ass beck here, Eddie, we need a bit of an assist.*"

"What?" Eddie said. "I thought I was strictly recon. Sort of trouble you got, what actual help could I possibly be?"

"*Get your fucking ass back here* now, *you little shit!*"

"Charming."

Eddie slewed the Testostorossa round in a handbrake turn he would have never believed he could do – and which, incidentally, had the Testostorossa calling him a total fucking maniac – and headed south.

As the Brain Train hove into view, Eddie caught on to what the problem was. A lucky shot from a shoulder-mounted launcher had breached a Behemoth tanker and it was leaking the coolant that kept the cargo refrigerated – and more importantly, kept the hydrogen-fusion processes of its power cell at an optimum operating temperature for not leaving a huge hole in the ground.

What kind of idiot, Eddie wondered, as the Loup obligingly dropped a sense of the mechanical schematics into his head, would tie the systems directly together? In any event, harassed as it was by Long Red motorsickles, the Behemoth was in no position to stop and effect repairs.

"*There's a shutoff valve on the linkage assembly,*" Trix Desoto told him via the comsat link. "*You have to get up there and shut the flow down manually.*"

"Oh yeah?" said Eddie. "And wearing a fucking tit for a hat I am."

"*What?*" Trix Desoto asked in what seemed like genuine puzzlement. "*What was that?*"

"Sorry," said Eddie. "That came out wrong. I don't quite know what I meant myself. The point is, what do I know about acrobatics on top of a speeding truck? Get one of the outriders to do it – they look like the sort who'll do any dumb thing for a laugh."

"Their job is to keep these jokers off you while you do yours. Besides, ever tried to stand up on a motorsickle while simultaneously pulling a lever that throws your balance off? Just do the *job*, okay?"

"No," said Eddie. "And you can't make me."

It occurred to him that was the wrong thing to say, to a woman who had control of a Leash that was, currently, the only thing that was preventing him from turning into a monster and exploding on a twelve-hourly basis.

Then again, so what? The important thing, here and now, was immediate survival from being crushed under the wheels of a loudmouth Testostorossa with a profound streak of homophobia and/or a Behemoth.

It was at this point that he felt the Testostorossa lurch. It slowed and segued in, then gunned the acceleration to match speeds and drive in tandem with the stricken Behemoth.

"The fuck?" Eddie exclaimed.

"*I'm taking control under Emergency Override,*" Trix said via the comsat link. "*It's locked in. The car itself couldn't change it, even if it meant going against the mission directives.*"

"And you're, like, totally fine with that?" Eddie asked the Testostorossa. "Totally surrendering all your individuality and volition and shit?"

"*Fine by me,*" the Testostorossa growled. "*The girl's a total babe and I like her. You, I don't care if you live or fucking die.*"

"I can just sit here," he said. "I can sit here and just do nothing. In fact, I think that's what I'll do. Or won't, if you get what I mean, and I'm sure that you do."

"*Hey, well, fine,*" said Trix Desoto over the satellite link. "*I've got two words for you. Ejector and seat.*"

Oh dear God," said Eddie. "You wouldn't. I mean, even GenTech wouldn't do something so cheesy and fucking stupid as fitting a car with an ejector seat, right?"

"*You'll never know,*" said Trix Desoto. "*Or at least — you'll know for about two seconds before your head hits the blacktop. So are you gonna do the job or what?*"

Eddie slithered into the shotgun seat and racked open the door. Scrambled up on to the roof of the Testostorossa and stood there in a semi-crouch.

It was easier, actually, than he had imagined. They were in the lee of the slipstream generated by the Behemoth and the air seemed, for the moment, still. And the Testostorossa's suspension was a dream – albeit the kind of dislocated and horrific dream from which you are desperate to wake up.

Willing himself into a the kind of terrified calm that has you moving very slow and sure in the knowledge that any sudden move might break the spell, Eddie turned to survey the tubes and cables of the Behemoth's linkage system that connected the cargo tanker to the cab. The shutoff lever for the coolant was plainly marked and visible – just well out of reach for someone who didn't have springs in his heels.

Eddie leaned in. Maybe he could get some purchase on the rig and haul himself over… and it was at this point that a Long Red zipped in around from the blindside, on a four-wheeled arrangement that seemed to consist of a pair of motorsickles lashed to either side of an aviation turbine, and levelled a sawn-off twelve-gauge directly at his head.

Then a GenTech outrider slammed in to broadside the Long Red, spearing him and his vehicle with the reinforced polycarbon blades that served both as impact-protection and offensive weapon – and which gave *motorsickles* their name as opposed to the more literal and prosaic *motorcycles*.

Presumably, the outrider had been counting in the impact-resistance aspect of those blades to protect him from damage – but those same blades now caught in the Long Red's mechanics and hauled the outrider over, sending both of them spinning off down the blacktop and on fire.

"Screw him," Eddie muttered to himself. "That's his job."

Now he realised that, in his alarm, he had just flung himself desperately into the Behemoth's connecting rig. He was hanging from a tangle of data-transfer cables, fortunately of the sort designed for rough and heavy duty treatment and thus could bear his weight.

The shutoff lever for the coolant was directly before him. He reached for it and yanked it.

The lever came off in his hand.

Eddie said a bad word.

Behind him, he heard a complicated, tearing crash as a number of vehicles collided in any number of interesting configurations. Eddie had no idea what had actually happened, and who might have died on either side, and quite frankly he didn't care.

The shutoff valve, despite the lack of a lever, still seemed more or less functional. Oh, well. It was worth a try. He grasped it with his free hand and attempted to twist it.

For a moment, it seemed that he was tearing the skin, and the meat for that matter, off his hand. Then, somehow, it was as if the skin and flesh had just hardened. The valve turned, then got a grip and lodged. Eddie Kalish had the distinct thought that he might have twisted it still further and torn it out, had he wanted.

In any case, he thought now, he'd done the job to any point of which he was capable – and if anybody like Trix Desoto, for example, wanted any more then they could just shove it.

Eddie let go of the cables, boosted himself off and dropped back into the Testostorossa, doing a neat little flip around the sill of the door that he would never know had looked incredibly impressive to anyone who might have seen it.

"All right," he said to the world in general. "I've fucking *done* it, okay? Good enough? Can I go, now?"

"*Good enough,*" the voice of Trix Desoto admitted over the comsat-link. "*For long enough.*"

The Testostorossa lurched again on its suspension.

"*I'm back under your masterful control,*" it said. "*You know, incidentally, just so's you know. So are you gonna drive me or what?*"

Eddie Kalish drove, running the last remaining Long Red off the road without even particularly thinking about it.

And it would only be later, yet again, that he realised that he had just done three separate things that it would have been impossible, for a human being, to do.

14.

After finishing off the Long Reds, the Brain Train hit nothing more than minor skirmishing. It was simply too big a target for any but the largest, well-supported or clinically insane gangcult to think it worth having a shot.

The Brain Train hit the Lone Pine ghoul-town and went through it slow, in silent running, while shark-like cars cruised the streets, driven by what appeared to be shapeless forms under sheets.

North through Bishop on Route 6, "Home of the World's Biggest Ball of Ear-wax!', only nobody wanted to see it. Then the State Line south of Boundary Park, where Trix Desoto decided to take advantage of the National Parks Service customs check to stop and repair the damaged Behemoth.

The net result was that, momentarily, Eddie Kalish found himself at a loose end. Masterton had given him a GenTech-issue credit chip – the first such thing he had ever owned – and it was burning a hole in his pocket.

The problem was that, here and now, there was nowhere and nothing to spend it on.

Eddie hauled the Testostorossa up next to a small convenience store a little way off from the Customs checkpoint. He debated with himself as to what might be the most expensive thing it stocked, but the exercise was probably pointless. He suspected he could buy the entire store, freehold, on GenTech credit.

A couple of girls, not wearing very much, were lounging by a vintage hydrogen-converted Caddy and chatting with a black guy in a long leather coat. They had Hollywood looks – that is, they looked how, in your dreams, hookers were supposed to look, as opposed to the way they actually do look in any real life.

One of the girls shifted round as he shot the door and clambered out of the Testostorossa.

"Hey, guy, nice ride," she said. "You feel like a good time?"

Eddie thought about this – and it must be said, he considered it in more or less the same terms you might consider going on a theme-park ride, or going to a movie. The unworldly perfection of these Californian girls was utterly at odds with, say, backroom girls in Las Vitas; it was difficult to think of them in the same connection.

"Yeah, sure," he said after a moment. "What do you do for a couple of grand?"

"We arrest you for soliciting," the black guy said, slapping a pair of smack-shackles around Eddie's wrists and then showing him his badge. California State Cavalry Vice Squad."

"The fuck?" Eddie bellowed. "This is entrapment!"

"No it isn't," one of the girls smirked. "We just asked you if you wanted a time. Didn't say a thing about money."

Much as he didn't want to make assumptions about good-looking girls – whether hookers or vice cops – and their general level of intelligence, Eddie got the distinct impression that this was the most brilliant trick that had ever been thought up, so far as she was concerned, and she wondered how anyone could have thought up such a brilliant trick.

"Okay, okay," he said wearily. "Write me a ticket or whatever. What's the fine?"

"Mandatory jail time," said the black guy. "Twenty-four hours."

"Shit," said Eddie, dispiritedly.

This altercation, meanwhile, had drawn the attention of Trix Desoto, who had left the roadside-maintenance of the damaged Behemoth and now stormed over.

"What's happening?" she demanded. "What's going on?"

The vice cops took one look at her, in her strategically-ripped PVC, and arrested her too.

"IDIOT!" TRIX DESOTO seethed. "You're an idiot. What are you? A fucking idiot, that's what you are."

"Sorry," said Eddie.

"I mean," Trix Desoto continued, "Nevada's famous for its legal prostitution industry. What on earth would have you trying to pick up hookers, two hundred yards the wrong side of the State Line? How could you not have realised it was a Moron Patrol?"

They were in the clean and otherwise empty cells reserved for those picked up by the State Cavalry Vice Squad – their lack of use testament to the fact that nobody was quite as stupid as Eddie Kalish.

It was all just a bit unfair, Eddie thought. In and of himself, he knew, he didn't know shit about anywhere much except for the little piece of New Mexico in which he had spent the majority of his life. It would have been nice if someone had thought fit to encode that particular bit of useful information into the Loup.

"I knew there'd be problems," Trix was saying, "the minute I heard we were heading into Nevada. I hate Nevada." She shuddered. "Too many bad memories."

"Memories?" Eddie said. "What memories?"

"None of your business."

"Suit yourself." Eddie sat on the fold-down cot and twiddled his thumbs.

"All right," Trix said after a while, in a somewhat exasperated voice, as though Eddie had dragged some revelation out

of her with his persistent and devilishly clever questioning. "I came out of one of the Nevada Baby Ranches."

"Baby Ranches?" Eddie said. The term meant nothing to him.

"It's one of the worst things that happened when the… Nevada Industry went out of control," Trix said. "Contraceptive failure is an occupational hazard, of course, and there were lots of ways for dealing with the result – but some of the worst operators simply dumped the results into internment camps, treated them like animals.

"It's like the way that, in Victorian London, you got orphanages – but you also got baby farmers, who took kids in exchange for the clothes on their backs, killed them and dumped the bodies in whatever the name is of that river they have over there." Trix got a brief far-away look in her eyes. Eddie realised that her own Loup was downloading some new bit of information for her. "The Thames."

Eddie supposed that he should be finding the whole idea of baby farming vaguely shocking. Then again, he'd been alive long enough to know the sort of shit people got up to, the sort of things they did to each other, so it wasn't exactly a big surprise.

"Bastards like that," he said, "strikes me that they'd be more likely to do what the baby farmers did instead of spending money even on a camp."

"Thank you for your concern," said Trix Desoto with withering sarcasm. "The Ranches were used to supply ready meat. Girls for the sickos who got off on torturing people to death. Fodder for the movies. I was picked up on a trawl by a Gen-Tech grey subsidiary operating in that area."

Trix smiled grimly.

"Fortunately, they ran a gene-scan before feeding me into the snuff-movie grinder. GenTech were on the look out for people with certain genetic markers – attributes that made them the perfect candidates for induction into what eventually became the Loup." She shrugged. "I got the first really viable strain. It's been tweaked a bit since then, but GenTech were nice enough to let me test out some of the preliminary effects on people I remembered from the Ranch. You know, guards and stuff."

"Does this Ranch still exist?" Eddie asked her.

Trix grinned. "What do you think? I was very thorough, apparently. So I'm told. This was before I learnt the techniques for riding the Loup and remembering what happened after."

For his part, Eddie Kalish was thinking that there was an aspect to Trix's story that was very interesting indeed. Masterton had never lost an opportunity to tell him, Eddie, how he had merely been some random body that had been infected with the Loup, purely on the basis that it had happened to be lying around.

Now, it seemed, there was an active search going on, on the part of GenTech, for those with the proper genome for the Loup to infect.

Eddie got the feeling that he was slightly more important in the general scheme of things than he had been told. This bore thinking about.

SOME HALF HOUR later, the black guy in the big leather coat came along and let them out.

"You been touched by an angel," he told them. "Seems like your bosses have a lot of swing with the California State Legislature. You've been sprung on your own recognisance."

"Word, motherfucker," said Eddie.

Trix Desoto looked at him. "You really can be a tool, can't you?"

"YOU'RE A FUCKING *idiot*," Masterton told him, over a scrambled signal on the Command and Control rig's comms link. "*What are you?*"

"I already told him," said Trix. "He's a fucking idiot."

"*You're not exactly in my best books either,*" Masterton told her. "*The Brain Train is supposed to be a covert operation, in so far as an enormous road-train rumbling down the pipe can be covert. That, for the hard of thinking, tends to mean that it is* not *a good idea to draw attention by getting arrested. And that goes double for you, Trix.*"

"Be fair," said Trix Desoto. "How was I to know about Attire Calculated to Promote Offence? They're statute-happy here in California, where the Law applies in the first place. Statutes about smoking within five hundred yards of a child, statutes

about taking the top off a bottle in an unsafe manner – and it changes on the hour. It's like they're compensating for all the places where they slit your throat over a clean syringe."

"*Be that as it may,*" said Masterton. "*You're on your last gasp. GenTech has too much invested in this particular operation to screw it up. Any more trouble, I yank the plug and we put together something else from scratch.*"

THE BRAIN TRAIN crossed into Nevada and dropped off the face of the world.

Tracksat-counterdetection systems were cut in. Radio silence was maintained. There was no way, short of being on the ground and watching it as it rolled past, that one could tell where it was and in which direction it was heading.

Except, of course, for the miniaturised tracer unit, planted by the Long Reds when they had attacked.

The tracker fed its data directly to the Long Red's backers, NeoGen, who extrapolated the Brain Train's route and learned that there was an upper-ninetieth percentile probability that its eventual destination was a location that did not appear, officially, on any map. Designation: Arbitrary Base.

Within NeoGen itself there was the feeling that the world would be a better place if they simply took the Brain Train out now. Stop messing around, just send in a strike-team and take them out from above.

Certain... associates, let us call them, however, countermanded the order. Their – call them adversaries – who were using GenTech as puppets, in much the same way that these associates were using NeoGen, wanted almost precisely the same thing as they did. Albeit to a somewhat different end.

Better, in the end, to let these GenTech minions do the job they had been appointed to do – and then come in at the last moment, and kill them all, and then enjoy the purloined fruits of their labours.

Besides, there were any number of other dangers still out there on the road. If the Brain Train fell prey to one of them, then all the labours of GenTech, and for that matter NeoGen,

and those who respectively backed them, would turn out to be absolutely meaningless in any case.

15.

BLACKOUT.

(Motherly, hushing sounds. The rasping slither of soft, warm skin.

Slipping crackle-crust. Soft, cool hands roll me over and a knee crunches into the back; sharp-edged carbon steel biting into wrists as hasps lock with quick precision: snick, snap.)

And we fade up to:

A clean bare room, cracks and patches of plaster crumbled off the lath.

Scrubbed floorboards. Abstract and vaguely totemic designs are scrawled on the walls: black and primitive but complex. Bright sunlight outside and a simple Japanese paper screen across the window. Black plastic bags of clothing strewn across the floor.

Scattered clothing, male and female.

A mattress lies against one wall. A radiator pipe and broken radiator. A small pile of various unused condoms in their wrappings by the bed. A ceramic bowl containing four used condoms beside it. There is blood on them; smears on the mattress.

A MAN, naked and face-down on the mattress, legs splayed and tied by ankles to steel rings bolted to the floor. His left wrist is handcuffed to the pipe. His right hand grips the pipe tightly. He wears a number of heavy rings.

There is a wad of bundled clothing under him, raising him slightly. Well defined musculature. Scratches fresh and half-healed on his back. A tattoo on his shoulder and another and another on his upper arm. A solid-black Cocteau design.

Longish, fine and off-blond hair. His face is pressed into the mattress. Straddling one splayed leg, on her knees, a WOMAN: mid-twenties, punkshock hair that might once have been blonde, face intent and childlike-serious.

(And in the Calibrian part of Italy, women saved a few drops of their menstrual fluid in a small bottle which they carried wherever they went. It was believed that when such drops were secretly administered to the man of their choice the man would be bound to them forever. The Elixir Rebeus!)

She smears her palm across her mouth. A slick film of saliva. She falls upon the man, gnaws gently on the back of his neck.

(And the weight on top of me, pressing on me, and a mouth pressed to my ear and murmuring.

She finally passed out. And when she finally passed out I hamstrung her, dislocated her hips and shoulders. It was vital that she remained immobile, absolutely still.

(Saline drips and bloodpacks. I inserted a catheter and I fed her through a needle. I kept her alive for months. It was quite difficult. Slaying skin and muscle and glucaea a single tiny shred at a time. A fragile tangle of veins and arteries and lymph ducts. Lymph and bile and cephalic fluid stored in individually-labled bottles and refrigerated. It's… You have to believe. Have to believe I never…

Her voice is cool and monotonic, matter-of-fact flipping someone I don't know from vanilla fem to ritual butchered meat. In that instant I don't know if she's making it up or not.)

She slithers down. Teeth clench lightly, momentarily and release. A tongue slips inside.

(There's a black iron engine hanging in a hot red sky and the machine is me and as I try to comprehend its vast and churning maze

of internal conduits my mind shifts and slips like shale and suddenly I crazy-move to:

Sand dunes under an azure summer sky. A salt breeze ripples samphire. A blonde and beautiful child, a girl, offers me a clump of tiny, pale blue flowers. It's not, she says, it's not — and the light, the crushing light comes down, washing out my field of vision with its flat blank white.)

Hooknails bite into shoulders and rake down. Slithers up: slugtrail tongue.

(And we stumbled through the tunnels 'til we found the husk of Nail: wasted and flaking and propped against the wall, crumbling into papergrey ash. The Strata Angel was there, a construct now, like gelid glass, shot with wormholes filled with lambent fluid. Shadowplay on translucent surfaces, macroforms splitting and flickering and pulsing. Somewhere somebody was shrieking, clawing at his face in a room of broken machinery…)

She half-smiles, catlike.

(She pirouettes in mid-air, screaming tactile subsonics from her eyes and mouth and vagina, down corridors and catwalks and vast brick vaults with chessboard floors and halls hung with shredded membrane and the false backs of cupboards and skylights and holes in the wall. A dark room hung with burning kites. The death of the hollow age.)

She shoves into him, digging nails into his back to afford purchase, and gouges down.

(An exquisite awareness of a slight mass under me. She's slipping faster now and I'm shuddering and—)

EDDIE KALISH JERKED awake.

He wasn't sure if something inside him had actively ejected him from the half-world of dreams — but he was damn glad that it had.

The dream had been so vivid that it recalled those he'd had while his brain was being physically rewired under the Loup. Information being downloaded from some actual other world, or from some future that might be, or some past that might have been if he… no, the details fled from him even as he tried to pin them down.

It was dark outside. He wondered if he had slept so long that he had missed one of his periodic inoculations with the Leash, thus explaining this sudden strength of his dreams. The Testostorossa's time readout told him, though, that he had several hours to go.

It wasn't so much that the dream had been unpleasant, he thought. Not as such. It had been like patching into a glimpse from some other actual life, one he might have had – now or in the future – if someone, or something, or anyone and everybody wasn't fucking him around in this one.

The end result was one of just feeling a mindless rage for having something taken away from you, without ever knowing precisely what it was.

The Loup, obligingly, dropped a piece of information into him. It was called an "involute" – a self-referring complex of ideas and images and emotions that lodges in the mind with such force that it seems more real than real, despite all evidence or logic. And in the hypnagogic state of waking up from sleep, Eddie was just having trouble working out what was real or not.

Ah, well. That explained everything then.

"*Had a nice sleep, then?*" the Testostorossa said, bringing Eddie instantly back to reality, or some reasonable approximation thereof. "*Dreaming about scamming on some guys, I'll bet.*"

Road signs swept past outside in an unreadable blur. Eddie didn't have the slightest idea of where he was.

The nature of running covertly meant that the Testostorossa was essentially now on autopilot, following a pre-programmed route. If they hit serious actual trouble then Eddie could override the controls and take them back to the Brain Train, but to all intents and purposes they were out of contact.

It was the sense of disassociation that was getting to him, Eddie thought – and when you came to think about it, that was slightly weird in itself. For most of his life Eddie Kalish had lived quite happily without much contact with other people at all.

Off to one side, through the Testostorossa window, the lights of some settlement or other hazed by, detached and drifting.

The quiet, smooth motion of the car under its state-of-the-art suspension, was hypnotic. Without being quite aware that he was doing so, Eddie drifted off to sleep again…

"So what are *we thinking?*" Masterton said over the comms-link. "*Are we thinking that he bought it?*"

"Yeah," said Trix Desoto, in the Brain Train Command and Control rig. "He bought it enough that he didn't get we were using the idea of a communications blackout to isolate him. Give the Loup in him some more time to do some deep-level restructuring."

She glanced at the readouts from the front-runner Testostorossa, which, despite anything Eddie Kalish might think, was in constant contact with the Brain Train. The read-outs were predominantly concerned with scans of Eddie's neural activity, picked up by sensors hidden in the headrest of the driving seat.

"He's developing quite the little personality in there," Trix said. "Should be something to see, you know – if it ever coheres and overtly evidences itself."

"*If?*" the voice of Masterton said. "*You're saying that even with this extra time, he won't be in a fit state to, uh, eat?*"

"It's just too little, too late," said Trix. "If you want my opin-ion. I really don't think he'll be ready when we hit the Base. We could try it, I suppose, but God only knows what a par-tially functioning memoplex might do. Could be worse than nothing."

"*How so?*" asked Masterton.

"Think of the differences between a skilled pilot at the stick of a Thunderstrike XIV, or nobody at all – or a brain-damaged moron flailing around every which way," said Trix. "Even nobody at all would be better."

"*I get your point,*" said Masterton, "*but nobody at all simply isn't an option. Our… associates are getting really insistent that we get this operation up and running as soon as possible. I'd hate to think what would happen if they get tired of waiting and decide to act directly, you know?*"

"Would we?" Trix asked. "Would we even know?"

"*Damned if I want to find out,*" said Masterton. "*Use the boy if you can, if there's any chance he's ready — but you know what you have to do if he isn't.*"

"Yeah," said Trix Desoto, grimly. "I know what I have to do."

16.

EDDIE WAS AWAKENED by a discreet chime from the dashboard HUD. At least, he would have been wakened by a discrete chime, had it not been drowned out by the Testostorossa shouting.

"*Wake up, fucker!*" the Testostorossa was bellowing. "*I got problems.*"

"What?" said Eddie. "What problems?"

"*Do you want the short explanation, or the technical one that'll leave your brain running out of your ears?*"

The thought crossed Eddie's mind that he could tell the Testostorossa to just go screw itself. There was nothing technical the Testostorossa could tell him that he wouldn't understand, with the possible exception of the radio, courtesy of the Loup.

Then again, he was just too tired. "Give me the short explanation."

"*A number of my fusion-compensatory systems have drifted out of alignment,*" the Testostorossa said. "*We need to get off the road and stop so I can run a self-diagnostic recalibration.*"

"What?" Eddie said. "Now, hang on, GenTech must have spent millions on you — you're telling me that, after all that, you have to stop for repairs after only a few hundred miles?

What sort of shitty quality control do they have back there at the factory?"

"*Hey, they made you, fucker, yeah?*" The Testostorossa's belligerence seemed a little defensive. "*I'm just saying that this is my first time out of the box, and there are some things you have to tweak when you're on the actual road. To a certain extent I'm still prototypical; this is a shakedown-operation in more ways than one. I need to get off the road for a while, and for some reason doing it isn't flagged as mission-critical — you have to tell me to do it.*"

Eddie thought about this. That was the first time he'd had the upper hand. The idea of cracking the electric whip, as it were, was a little bit tempting.

"Supposing I say no?" he asked. "Purely for the sake of argument, you understand."

"Ever seen a hydro-fusion explosion from ground zero?" the Testostorossa said.

"Do it!" Eddie snapped. "Do it now!"

The Testostorossa segued off onto a slip road and ramped its power down, gliding to a halt.

"Is this gonna take long?" Eddie said. "Cause I'm telling you I don't like this. We're out of contact with the Brain Train, stuck alone in the middle of nowhere and — oh fuck. There's something up there."

Off to the side of the road, firelight and the bulky, silhouetted forms of vehicles.

"Just my luck," Eddie muttered to the Testostorossa. "You go wrong just in time to drop us in the middle of a gangcult camp."

Uncharacteristically, the Testostorossa remained silent. Presumably it was devoting its run-time to performing the self-diagnostics it had mentioned.

Eddie fired up the microcams and cut in the image-enhancement. The monitor showed a collection of parked vehicles ranging from ancient pickup trucks to sixteen-wheeler RVs, daubed with cruciforms and what Eddie recognised as Burning Hearts and what, he presumed, were quotations from the Bible.

This latter presumption was confirmed by the HUD, which ran the configurations and attempted to pull an ID from its database. All it came up with was UNKNOWN and a potential threat-factor of, likewise, UNKNOWN.

"Shit," said Eddie.

He was left with two choices. He could just sit there and pray that nobody noticed him, or leave the car and try to get a handle on what was going on.

After maybe twenty minutes, however, Plan A began to pall. It was the sheer uncertainty that was the worst thing; sitting in the dark and waiting for God knew what to fall on him. At length, Eddie eased open a door and snuck towards the firelight, taking advantage of what ground-cover he could.

EDDIE MADE HIS cautious way around the bulk of a bulky sixteen-wheeler, wondering what gangcult-related horrors might meet his eyes. In the event, and horrific enough in its own way, he was utterly unprepared for a bunch of bearded, bespectacled freaks in jumpers, sitting around a campfire, strumming on guitars and singing "Kumbaya".

And, as the old joke goes, that was just the women.

Actually, he saw, as his eyes accustomed themselves to the new lighting conditions with Loup-accelerated speed, that was just the group around the campfire that just happened to be near him. Around other fires, dotted around the patch of desert corralled by the various RVs, there were other figures.

There was a confusing mix of attire and demeanour, but each of the people seemed to be what Eddie vaguely thought of as religious types. Prim church-ladies and Lutheran pastors rubbed shoulders and broke bread with ascetic and somewhat ragged figures in monk robes that looked more like what Rasputin would have worn – as opposed to those worthy Trappists who brew delicious beer to the glory of God, the aid and benefit of the Walloons, and walk in truth and beauty all their days.

In fact, these robed figures seemed… not out of place exactly, but more definite and distinct than all the other

religious types. In every group, they seemed to be the centre of attention. It was as if they had been imposed on the others, in the sense of stripping some new element into a photograph, and were guiding them.

Shepherding was the word, Eddie supposed.

"Greetings, brother," said a voice behind him. "And how might we assist you this fine night?"

Eddie nearly swallowed his tongue. There was just no way that someone could have come up from behind him like that, not with his well-known rat-line, and not to mention Loup-enhanced, senses alert for danger.

He turned to see one of the thin robed figures. It was as if the man had simply materialised out of thin air.

"I've, uh," Eddie said, "I had a bit of car trouble. Nothing to worry about, it's being... and then I saw your fires."

"'A decided boon against the chills of the desert night,'" said the man. "Father Barnabas at your service. Might I invite you to warm yourself, a little, before going on your way?"

"Uh..." Eddie didn't have anything much against the religious types of the world; he didn't bother them so long as they didn't bother him. But there was something about this Father Barnabas that just creeped him out. He seemed entirely affable and harmless on the surface – but Eddie got the distinct impression that was what it was. The face was absolutely composed in a friendly smile, but there could be anything behind it.

Of course, Eddie's unease might have been due to the small fact that all those gathered here – every single one – had stopped their guitar-playing and breaking bread and whatever else the fuck it was they had been doing, and had silently turned towards him with similarly fixed and gnomic smiles.

Eddie wondered about that, too, until the Loup supplied the information that the word "gnomic" had nothing whatsoever to do with gnomes.

"Hey, listen," he said. "I don't want to... say, who are you guys, anyway?"

"Josephites, for the most part," said Father Barnabas. "A small cross-denominational sect, to be sure, but gaining some

small degree of significance of late." He gestured to take in the assembled multitude. "As it is, we are currently on our way to Utah, there to gain admittance to a certain seclusionary at the behest of our great leader. I have, myself, made a small hymnal to this most wondrous endeavour…"

Eddie became aware that the gathered multitude – every single one of them – had begun to hum sonorously, as though in preparation for a rendition of an entirely different nature from an inept and sappy perpetration of "Kumbaya". There was a low solemnity to the voices that spoke of absolute and fervent seriousness.

And, now, they began to sing:

"Ohhh… we're off to see the Elder,
The glorious Elder Seth!
We hear he's built a whiizz of a place
And called it Deseret…"

Eddie felt it was time he made his excuses and left.

"Hey, it's been fun," he began, "but I really must be…"

"Oh but I *insist* that you join us," said Father Barnabas, a new light of intensity igniting in his eyes, in the sockets of the smiling mask of his face. "For a while, at the very least. And, who knows, when you hear the Good News we have to offer, and hear it for long enough, perhaps you'll be *amenable* to –"

It was at that point that the Testostorossa powered itself up with a blaze of headlamps and a roar. It powered towards Eddie and Father Barnabas and spun to halt, racking open a door.

"I'm up and running," it growled. *"Get your kicks sucking men in dresses off some other time, yeah?"*

"Fuck you, you prototypical piece of shit," snapped Eddie. And it must be said that he said it with a small sense of relief.

A second before he had been pinioned by the eyes of Father Barnabas; now it was as if some spell had been broken.

"It's been, uh, real, you know?" he said to the somewhat nonplussed Father Barnabas, hauling the door shut. "Catch you in the church newsletter funny pages."

* * *

"SO WHO WERE *those jerks, anyway?*" the Testostorossa demanded as they swung back out onto the main highway. "*There's a bunch-of-jerks shaped hole in my database and I don't like it.*"

"Just this bunch of religious whackos," Eddie told it shortly. He really needed to get some sleep. "Josephites, they called themselves, heading on to some loon-factory called Deseret. It's not important. No big deal."

It would only be later, and elsewhere, that he would learn the truth about how wrong he was – and how close his escape, here and now, had been.

THE NEXT TIME Eddie woke, without remembered dreams of any kind, it was to find the Testostorossa sitting inside what appeared to be a military compound, with various US Cavalry troops surrounding him. They were on the point of lowering their guns, which had previously been aimed directly at him through the Testostorossa's windshield.

Behind him the Brain Train was rumbling through the perimeter gates, the Behemoths fanning out to take up parking-position on a parade ground which had probably been someone's pride and joy of order before getting churned up by Behemoth wheels.

A few minutes later, when she came over to deliver the latest shot of the Leash, Trix Desoto told him that the Testostorossa had come slewing in through the perimeter on pre-programmed autopilot out of the blue. And it had only been someone on the Brain Train remembering to break communications-silence, and inform Arbitrary Base of their arrival, that had prevented him from being summarily taken out as a potential terrorist suicide bomber.

On the whole, Eddie was slightly more relieved than otherwise that he had been asleep for the whole thing.

final quadrant
arbitrary base

AND THEN, FROM an open window beyond the bed, a roscoe coughed "Ka-chow!"… I said, "What the hell – !" and hit the floor with my smeller… A brunette jane was lying there, half out of the mussed covers… She was as dead as vaudeville.

"Brunette Bump-off"
Spicy Detective
May 1938

suppLemantary
data: fiLe retrievaL

[THE FOLLOWING EXCERPTS *are from a pgp-secure email sent from one Dexter Corncrake, a so-called "Research Consultant" – read free-lance cracker – for the New York Times, to Detective Inspector Ronald Craven of the NYPD Missing Persons Unit on 07/06/2005. See relevant NSA-intercept archives. These excerpts are provided FOR BACKGROUND-INFORMATIONAL PURPOSES ONLY, on the basis that subsequent dormanting of both Corncrake and Craven fall outside the remit of this agency. No further action required.*]

I'M GONNA PRINT this out and then I'm gonna zero the hard-drive and burn my notes and then just try to forget about this whole shitty mess. It probably won't do any good; there's probably a quiet little transponder bug, on the lowest level of the operating system, discreetly reporting every keystroke back to its masters even as I type. I'm telling you, I've never really thought of myself as a coward, but all this is just too–

I'VE MADE UP this guy in my head and called him Stanley – just like the psychotherapist from that godawful book about multiple personalities. (I mean, the bitch had supposedly sixty-four

separate automemes operating, one of whom was apparently this, like, total literary genius on the level of Shakespeare or Joyce. So why didn't *he* write it, instead of bringing in some schlock-hack crap who wouldn't know connected prose if it crawled up his, her, its or their collective backside?)

Anyhow. I've made up this guy in my head and called him Stanley, and I'm going to write this to him, in the hope that I don't let anything slip about, well, you, even by implication. That all right there, Stanley? Are you sitting down comfortably? Then let us begin:

Federal-based systems were like this total dead end. The clearance procedure overrides were built right into the hardware when the Central Registry was consolidated. Utterly integral to it. *Any* ID-check flagged as "Special Services Section Eight" comes up clean, no actual data-exchange involved save for some rather high-powered context checking to preclude the obvious confusion with servicemen being invalided from the armed services on the grounds of mental health.

No joy with the old NSA either – until I took off the time-lock and trawled back through the trash logs of the dormanted stuff. The stillborn junk that never got off the ground in the first place, so never needed to be capped at the end…

Long story short, I found a way in.

There's some *weird* shit back there, Stanley. Did you know, for example, that back in the Eighties there was a serious proposal to covertly modify the TV receivers of certain notable left-wing militants so they pumped out hard X-rays through the cathode? The intention, simply, was to increase the number of cancer deaths among left-wing firebrands.

The project foundered when some bright spark realised that left-wing firebrands, as a group, tend to watch a lot less TV than the population as a whole.

Whole lot of stuff like that – some of it even going as far back as 1945 and the reports of death camp experimentation unearthed during the Liberation. And some of these are front-reffed to our old friends Special Services Section 8 and something called the Janus Program. Janus was, of course, the

Keeper of the Gate and such crap. The god of doors and portals – go and look it up in a book on comparative mythology if you even care.

The Janus Program was set up maybe thirty years ago and ran for about ten, based in and operating from a number of disused sewers and maintenance-tunnels running roughly parallel with the Greater Metropolitan Subway. Various plans and schematics attached. There are references to a Bunker of some kind – always capitalized – but I was never able to track it down definitively. I've marked one or two most likely locations on the plans attached.

I also found specs for some seriously heavy duty processing equipment, apparently based upon optical-switching technology – years ahead of its time.

Who the controllers of the concern were, who its operatives were, of their aims and objectives and ultimate remit, I still have no idea. I've found the skeletons of personnel files, salary scales and so forth, that allow me to hazard some basic guesses on the overall picture, but every hard-data specific has been wiped.

One thing, however, is abundantly clear, from working back from the gaps and looking at the shapes the holes make. They were experimenting on kids, Stanley. Kids procured by a seemingly random process of informing mothers that their infants had been stillborn and then just spooking them away. More than seven thousand of them over the course of a decade.

Exposing them to something. Infecting them with something. With what, precisely, and to what purpose, I have no idea. Again, there are skeleton records to suggest that the effects of this infection, whatever it was, were studied over a period of years, but no hard data remain.

Whatever the nature of the infection was, the mortality rate was high, running from seventy-five percent at the start to maybe fifty percent by the end.

Those who survived, and were old enough by this point to remember the procedures, were given post-hypnotic blocks

and reintroduced to the general population by way of foster homes and adoption services. It's not outside the bounds of possibility to imagine that a number of mothers got their supposedly deceased infants back under a new guise.

In any case, Stanley, it struck me that these kids are now old enough to have children of their own. That got me thinking, so I ran some comparisons and extrapolations from such data as remains extant.

Your missing kids, Stanley, the disappearances you're investigating, are the children of the Janus Program subjects.

I think somebody, somewhere is covering his tracks. Like I said, the background material on this thing goes as far back as the death camps – and like the death camps, I suspect that all of this was done for no consistent or coherent reason at all. It was done for the simple reason that someone could do it and get away with it.

It hasn't ended, Stanley. It hasn't stopped. The disappearances of the kids, the murders in [section deliberately defaced from source] are just the visible tip, for the simple reason that this was where the victims were most concentrated. Is the same thing happening, to some less noticeable extent, throughout the entire country? The entire world ..?

This is all too big for me, Stanley. It's just too big. I said I'd never thought of myself as a coward, but I've been lying awake nights, just wondering what people with those kind of resources – people capable of even countenancing these things – are capable of doing to me.

You, too, Stanley. My advice to you is to drop it. Leave it alone and walk away. Find yourself a rock or something and crawl under it and hide.

They're just going to do this, and do it, and keep on doing it – and you can try to pretend it's not happening or you can stand in their way and let them roll right over you.

There's just no way you're ever going to stop it.

radio none

"This is WWAXXZY News, every hour, on the hour. But first, an important message from the First Evangelical Church of PractiBrantics…

"There's so much neat stuff you can do with your Ka. There's lots of stuff to do. But first, of course, you have to release its awful mystic power.

"In olden times you had to trepan yourself and peel back your skull with a claw hammer, something that only the bravest of Ancient Visionaries could countenance themselves to do, what with the influence of Evil Humours, prehistoric germs and all.

"Now, at last, there is an easy way, with the FIRST EVAN-GELICAL CHURCH OF PRACTIBRANTICISM.

"(Don't let the name fool you. PRACTIBRANTICS is a well known and respected Science, respected by such Scientists as Albert Einstein, Gallileo, Planck and Dr Leonard Troll-trundler – the inventor of the chrononambulatory ambulator, the inflatable goitre and the galvanistic cheese drive himself!

"The FIRST EVANGELICAL CHURCH OF PRAC-TIBRANTICISM is classed by US Law as a religion, purely

so our funds can be channelled into the areas where it does most good, rather than diverted to its own ends by a Government composed of those without the Enlightenment that comes from even the most basic MENTAL FLENSING.)

"Once our highly trained technicians hook you to the patent-pending FLENSING BOX and flood your brain with the healing purple power of orgone energy, the true potential of you Ka will be released – the mystic twinkling entity that exists within us all, and has done so for trillions upon trillions of centuries. Immortality awaits YOU – not a moment too soon! And here's *why*…

"Dr Trolltrundler himself, in his fine and Scientific data-wafer *The Last Body in the Shop: How PRACTIBRANTICS Can Help You Keep It*, that what with the demographic time bomb, impending Catastrophic Climactic Shift and with half the male population of the world functionally sterile due to cumulative endocrine contamination, there will soon be too few human bodies to go around. People will have to share, or come back as rocks, or be transplanted into such monstrous forms of solid-state cybernesis and cultured fungus that it would drive them mad. Do you hear me? Mad!

"Is this a risk you are prepared to take for yourself? For your loved ones? Of course not. So call this number and learn the FACTS. It's the most important call you'll make in this or any other lifetime.

"Send no money now. Our flying PARAPRACTIBRAN-TIC team will be more than happy to deal with such trifles when they arrive at your door…"

"And our top story of this cycle must be the tragic collapse of the Golden Gate Bridge, killing seventy-five thousand. The death-count is so high because this once-historic construction was at the time blockaded by a coalition of demonstrators protesting US involvement in the Congolese War.

"We here at WWAXXZY News fully support freedom of speech and the expression of ideas of all kinds, however repug-nant they might be to right-thinking citizens of this great country of ours.

"We have to ask, though, in the light of such an appalling tragedy – should we not be thinking of curtailing the free expression of ideas to gatherings of no more than, say, three men and a dog? We here at WWAXXZY News say yes, and if Amendment 7054 is passed, you won't be able to say anything other than yes either.

"What makes the atrocity doubly vile, White House sources say, is that there are strong suggestions that it can be traced to Congolese-backed terrorists themselves, loosening the cables, as opposed to simple faulty maintenance. Despite the White House's statement, rumours are already circulating some of the more scurrilous datanet sites that it may actually have been carried out by rogue elements within our very own government. The conspiracy theory goes that they wanted to kill two birds with one stone by inflaming the Congolese situation and removing opposition in one fell swoop.

"The terrorists responsible are still at large. They could be anywhere. They could be anyone, even people known to you. Stay in your homes. Stay off the streets. Stay in your blocks. Report any suspicious activity – any activity at all – to representatives of your local officially designated Black Squad.

"In other news, the body of controversial rap music, action figure and sex industry entrepreneur Big Master X was found floating in New York's Hudson River today. Although a suicide note was found pinned to his body, the boys at NYPD Inc. are refusing to rule out foul play. Our love and thoughts go out to the family and friends of Big Master X during this difficult time. To read the suicide note in full, log into the WWAXXZY datanet using the keyword 'floatingfatboy' and remember to have your cashplastic at the ready.

"And on a lighter note, old William Hicks is at it again. Originally intended to address the Golden Gate rally himself, the senator was discovered last night, wandering Times Square in New York, without his trousers and muttering that he had seen proof that both the US Government and the Multicorps are colluding to cover up the fact that we are all of us living in a recursive virtual reality which vast and

unimaginable Entities from outside space and time are playing like a game.

"Well, if that were true, it's certainly game over for Mr
Hicks in this presidential race. Relentless indeed, Bill.

"That was WWAXXZY News, every hour, on the hour.
And now, in memory of Big Master X, we're devoting the rest
of the afternoon's programming to some of the best music
released on his Big Black Beats label starting with his very
own remix of Freak-E's 'Be My Pimp'…"

17.

THE SCOPE OF Federal Government, as an instrument of power, might have atrophied; the might of Multicorporations might be split as the individual corporate concerns squabbled amongst themselves for the prize of the world – but the California National Guard (or Arnie's Freedom Commandos, as certain sectors of the corporate media had dubbed them) were still going strong.

Admittedly, the California state legislature had banned them from operating within their home state but they had enough rich backers among the tech and entertainment industries to buy themselves bases in all of the neighbouring states, ready to strike at a moment's notice should law and order in California break down completely. Add this to Governor Arnie's statewide draft programme and the US Army spreading its forces across almost a hundred nations worldwide, and the California National Guard becomes the most powerful military force in North America. Only a few private corporate armies and southern gangcults come anywhere close in terms of both man and firepower and, the California state legislature notwithstanding, there was nobody to challenge their military dominance.

There were any number of reasons for this. Some to do with the functions a well-armed and well-trained military force performed and the responsibilities it had within a chaos-bound overall social dynamic. Others to do with the fact that the CNG's presence in sympathetic states dissuaded gangcults, terrorists and other assorted whackos from attacking government, corporate and private interests there. Others still to do with their favoured status within the Pentagon and the multitude of homeland security contracts they were awarded by the top brass there. But chief among those reasons must be counted the simple and obvious one that they had a shitload of heavy weaponry, and who was going to take it away from them?

So, foreign wars were still waged and police actions still fought to protect the interests of America but homeland security, unofficially at least, fell under the remit of the CNG.

Johnny Raghead still got the crap kicked out of him before being shipped off to Kandahar, Guantanamo or Diego Garcia if he even so much as looked at a subway air conditioning unit. God-fearing patriots in the northern militias and survivalist groups would get a jackboot up their collective asses anytime they refrained from paying their Federal taxes. ICBMs remained maintained in their various silos and racks. Bomb testing was still conducted – and certain complications attendant to bomb testing, on a whole other level than mere fallout, were still, after a fashion, dealt with.

This latter function fell under the remit of what, over the years, had come to be called Arbitrary Base.

COLONEL ROLAND GRIST, Commander in Charge of Arbitrary Base, surveyed the pair of GenTech so-called "civilian specialists" across the expanse of his desk. He was not exactly impressed.

The girl was wearing something in skin-tight PVC that left nothing to the imagination but which, even so, was strategically ripped to leave even less so. With her bleach-blonde hair and overplayed cosmetics she looked like she'd be more at home sliding round a pole.

For all this, she radiated assurance, a sense that if she happened to decide a direction in which the world would go, then the world would fall into line as a matter of suit. Grist was reminded, a little disquietingly, of a nanny employed by his family back when he was growing up on their Cape Cod compound. The girl had done drugs and spent most afternoons screwing his father – but so far as little Roland had been concerned, her word had been strict and absolute law.

The boy was just what the word "boy" implied: a kid around the age of the youngest grunts under Grist's command, without even the most basic of the training that would have him straightened up and flying right.

The boy was twitchy and pale, hunched sullenly in a gangcult leather jacket several sizes too big for him; shadowed eyes glowering up at Grist under a straggled mass of hair that had long since crossed the border from being merely greasy into the country of the positively matted with filth.

He looked most definitely like a drug addict, this boy – and you could pick any drug you liked, it would probably fit.

For himself Grist couldn't imagine this pair making it through the Base perimeter alive in normal circumstances, let alone being allowed into the more sensitive areas.

Pentagon orders, however, had been quite clear. They were to be given the run of the place, given any assistance or information for which they might ask, whether that meant launch-codes for the SNARK XIV's in their silo-racks... or access to the so-called "Artefact" in Shed Seven.

The bureaucrats in the Pentagon were watching him, Grist knew. They were watching him all the time, just to see if he would fumble the ball again. There were Special Forces operatives on the Base that he still had not properly identified, at least to the point where he could be certain where their loyalties truly lay.

He was not in a position, at this point, to blatantly disobey direct orders from above.

He didn't know how many of his men were in on the joke.

All the same, there was nothing in the orders telling him to make the job of these two easier. If this pair wanted anything, they had to know what to ask and then damn well ask it.

"Sir, ma'm," he said, the honorifics of respect all-but sticking in his craw. "Our sponsorship arrangement with GenTech Industries requires that we offer you any assistance you might require. I can have a maintenance crew go over your rigs, have you on your way in—"

"Any one of your guys lays a hand on our rigs," said the girl, "at this point and without clearance, is going to be chopped down instantly. This isn't the pit-stop, this is the finish line."

Grist remained impassive. He'd guessed from when they had told him that the convoy was coming that they weren't going to just be using Arbitrary Base as a maintenance way station; this was just a way of letting this pair know that he was going do to nothing more or less than they actively asked.

"What we're going to need," said the girl, actively telling rather than asking for anything, "is your tech-support team scrambled and ready to go. Nobody under Stratum XIV clearance, and you'll better believe we're going to be checking the list, and checking it twice, from our own database.

"Step up the perimeter guard, and they can be cleared to any level you like – just keep them away from all GenTech personnel and what they're doing. Plus we're going to need a squad of Special Forces Deltas as an escort while we set up shop in the place you dammed well know that we will."

Grist still remained impassive, biting on the polycarbon tube replacing the cigars to which, in off hours and in the open air, he was partial.

"And that would be?" he said.

"Where do you think?" said the girl. "Shed Seven."

"So LET ME get this right," Eddie said as they headed through the Arbitrary Base compound, watching various military personnel snapping to order in the way that only military personnel can do. "This is what…" He racked his brain for the half-remembered UFO mythology he had picked up growing

up in New Mexico – where they had a lot, admittedly, but of a sort that set off so many bullshit detectors that you never bothered to even learn it. "This is what they used to call Area 51 or something, yeah?"

Trix Desoto snorted. "Stop being a tool. You've been quite the tool for long enough and it's been mentioned before. Area 51 never existed. The whole idea of it was fabricated to draw attention away from the things that were really going on."

"Oh yeah?" said Eddie. "So what really happened?"

"Don't ask," said Trix. "Just remember, some shit goes down and you hear that things called greys are involved, be very, very afraid. Little bastards aren't nearly so harmless as they try to make out. This isn't about that."

Eddie wasn't entirely sure that Trix was joking. She gestured to take in the prefabricated barracks huts and storage units of the Base.

"Arbitrary Base," she said, "is basically a moveable feast; the facilities that make it what it is, that allow it to deal with what it deals with, move between the existing installations, patching into their command structures…"

"You seem to know a lot about this stuff," Eddie said. "Gen-Tech's really running Arnie's Freedom Commandos? Is that how it is?"

"We wish," said Trix Desoto. "It's a hangover from the whole Military-Industrial Complex thing. That whole self-perpetuating thing of selling a bunch of arms to guys, then sending in our guys to sort out the situation where you've got a bunch of armed guys, you know?

"Anyhow. The Pentagon is split up into as many factions as there are Multicorps, these days. GenTech just happened to end up connected with the faction running Arbitrary Base." She smiled sardonically. "Lucky for us."

"Oh yeah?" said Eddie. "How so?"

"How so because certain of our… associates have a serious interest in the materials falling under the remit of Arbitrary Base. Or maybe it was the other way around: GenTech had

access to those materials, which is why our… associates made contact with us in the first place."

It might have been all the new knowledge downloaded into him as a part of his induction into the Loup, but Eddie was learning to recognise an ellipse at twenty paces.

"And so just who, exactly, are these dot, dot, dot *associates?*" he asked.

"You'll find out," said Trix Desoto. "For the moment, though, initially, it's gonna be better to show than tell. And here we are. Shed Seven."

A squad of Deltas were waiting for them outside of an unprepossessing galvanised steel hut.

Eddie had occasionally come across off-duty military out in Las Vitas, and so some large part of him expected to be greeted with, at best, outright hostility. A supercharged Testostorossa had nothing on off-duty military when it came to assuming that people with more brains than muscle were fags.

Not that he'd had any brains to speak of in the first place, he recalled, which had left him doubly screwed.

He assumed that Trix Desoto herself might be made, well, *welcome*, for a certain number of reasons, but not in an entirely salutary manner.

Now he came to appreciate the difference between highly trained and not, and off-duty and on. The soldiers snapped to instant attention as he and Trix approached, and the lieutenant in charge of them saluted.

"Butcher," he said, matching the name tag on his greens.

Eddie thought of several replies to that, but then discounted them more or less instantly as either heavy handed or asinine. A guy in the CNG with the name of *Butcher* would have heard them all in any case.

"You requested a close-order escort," said Butcher. It came out as a kind of completely neutral statement, requiring neither confirmation not comment.

"Yeah," said Trix Desoto, confirming it anyway. "Don't sweat it, There's no rush; we just want to check it out at this point. You'll have time to get into your gear."

"Ma'm," Butcher said.

It might have been Eddie's imagination, but there seemed to be a sense of relief, both in Butcher and his squad, though they gave absolutely no external sign.

The escort took them into Shed Seven. Eddie had not been quite sure what to expect – but he certainly hadn't expected it to be bare-walled and completely empty.

"What *is* this–" he began, when the floor lurched under him and dropped with the whine of heavy-duty servos.

Eddie wasn't entirely stupid – at least, since undergoing the processes of the Loup it seemed to him that he was increasingly less so – so by the time the servos whined down to a stop he had more or less convinced himself that his underwear was safe.

They were in an underground chamber slightly larger than the galvanised hut of Shed Seven had been. Along one wall were racked the bulky and somewhat ape-like forms of heavy-radiation armour.

At an order from Butcher, the squad broke formation and began climbing into the suits double-time. Eddie noted that, for all their speed in doing so, they were extremely careful about checking the on-board systems and seals.

Trix Desoto, meanwhile, had wandered over to a storage unit, from which she now returned with a pair of paper-thin polyceramic coveralls.

"There you go," she said, giving one of them to Eddie.

Eddie looked down at it. The cuffs at the wrists and ankles seemed to be elasticated.

"The fuck?" he said.

"What do you think?" said Trix Desoto. "You want Mommy's help putting it on the right way round or something?"

"Yeah, but…" Eddie gestured in the direction of soldiers busily girding themselves up for any and all manner of radioactive nastiness.

"Oh, right," said Trix Desoto. "The coverall isn't to protect *you*. Nobody cares what happens to *you*, frankly. We're going

into a clean environment. I'd advise you to look up the term,
along with the word 'soap'."

THE SHED SEVEN-SIZED elevator floor lurched again. Eddie
decided that this was probably because it was built to military
specifications as opposed to faulty design. It was built to do the
job, and do it reliably, rather than indulge in the niceties of
giving a smooth ride.

"This is gonna have to be refitted," said Trix Desoto. "Some
of the components we're going to be bringing down here are
a little too... delicate for all this lurching around."

"That was a polite way of putting it," said Eddie.

He was not in a particularly good temper. The elasticated
band around the polyfabricated hair-cap he was wearing
seemed to be increasingly cutting into his head.

"I was trying for elliptical, myself," said Trix Desoto.

Like Eddie, she was now in cap and coveralls – though the
latter were a strategic half a size too small for her, to noticeable aesthetic effect. An effect periodically enhanced by the
blasts of air that washed over them as the butterfly wing
hatches of airlock stations slammed shut above.

"So, Eddie," said Trix Desoto in a loud, clear voice. "You
ever seriously think about getting it *on* with me?"

The question, coming completely out of left field, left Eddie
momentarily dumbfounded, as though several areas of his
brain had simply and physically shorted out.

"I mean, I know what I come off like in my... with my
usual look." Trix Desoto glanced sidelong at a collectively and
absolutely stone-faced squad of Deltas, what could be seen of
their faces behind their visors.

"Couple of guys here," she continued, "are having a little bit
of difficulty keeping their fingers on their numbers. And
you're, what, seventeen years old? You should be getting a little
chubby on over the thought of dry wall. Thinking up things to
try and talk to me about. Looking for excuses to touch me and
cop a feel." She turned to look at him meaningfully. "And I just
don't get any of that from you, Eddie. I wonder why."

Of any possible scenario while being stuck in an elevator with a squad of Delta-trained Marines this was absolutely, in the considered opinion of Eddie Kalish, the very worst.

"My age?" he managed, latching on to one desperate detail in an attempt to head the conversation off. "You're maybe two years older than I am…"

"Yeah, well girls notoriously mature faster than boys," said Trix Desoto. "So you're shafted twice, and not in a good way, believe you me. Don't you *like* girls, Eddie? Is that it? Do you prefer boys?"

Not *absolutely* the very worst thing he could have imagined, then.

"Could I borrow your gun, please," he said to Lieutenant Butcher. "I think I'd like to shoot myself in the head."

A second later, a slightly bemused Eddie Kalish was looking down at his hand, in which was held the automatic pistol which the lieutenant had instantly unclipped from the side of his radiation armour and had given to him.

"Good job you didn't ask him to do the job for you," said Trix Desoto, a little sardonically. "You wouldn't believe your current clearance so far as these guys are concerned."

Eddie handed the gun back to Butcher, who racked it back onto his rad-armour without comment.

"The reason I bring it up," said Trix Desoto, "is that there are a number of people out there, you know, out there in the world, with a specific and particular variety of Alienation Syndrome."

She pronounced the term in a way that you could hear the capitalisation.

"The effect's quite subtle," she continued. "It's very easy to confuse with merely having a touch of Asberger's, or Adoptive Syndrome – you know, dislocated from any family with a similar genetic makeup – or just being, basically, a bit of a sad little dork who's a failure in everything and who doesn't have any friends.

"The symptoms include a total failure to understand how humans can go crazy for things, any number of things – for a

girl or a boy, or for money, or for a leader giving orders. A certain lack of concern for other human beings and what happens to them, however bad. There's a connection simply broken in there.

"These people always seem to have murky and displaced origins – like foundlings, you know? But whereas most displaced persons tend to spend their lives trying to find out who they are and where they came from, searching out living relatives and trying to go home, that sort of thing just never even so much as occurs to these people…"

Eddie, for his part, was starting to wish that Trix Desoto would go back to digging at him about his sexuality. At least such jibes could be defended against by a general and generic response.

This specific detailing of his character and its flaws, on the other hand, was just hurtful.

"Well pardon me for living!" he snapped. "Okay, so I don't know exactly where I came from before, I dunno, the first places I remember being and the first things I remember doing. Forgive the *fuck* out of me for not tearing my hair out all the live-long day and wailing about It!"

"Hey, I'm just saying," said Trix, "that some people just don't have the homing-instinct. They don't have it because they *know*, on the deep subconscious level, that to have one would be completely and utterly pointless. There's nowhere in the world for them to go."

The elevator platform gave another lurch.

"I think we're coming to the end of the line," said Trix. "Don't take what I just said to heart. I've been trying to prepare you a little, just so's you don't go completely batshit on me. And a second from now, you'll see what I mean…"

ABRUPTLY, THE SEQUENCE of butterfly wing hatches slamming shut behind them became a single armoured hatch locking into place in a rock ceiling. The elevator platform rack-and-pinioned down support pylons through a cavern.

The cavern was not impossibly vast, just bigger than the mind was comfortable with.

Visitors to the ventilation galleries of coal mines, or to the overly grandiose subway stations of the world, have reported just that vertiginous sensation: it's not that this empty subterranean space is big, but that it's obviously man-made, imposed on the bedrock of the world, and so feels somehow wrong.

Or if not man-made then at least artificial – and one can ponder that particular distinction later.

Concrete stanchions reinforced the rock walls in the manner of the support superstructure of a cathedral dome. Their undressed surfaces seemed to have been colonised by some strange fungoid organism: fleshy webs of tendrils from which cilia rippled like the soft spines of a sea urchin; clusters of globular fruiting-members that by some inner process appeared to give off their own light. Clusters of jewels sprouting in flesh.

The fungus might or might not have been found anywhere else on Earth, but Eddie recognised it. If you took into account all the screwing around that dreams do, where you can go to sleep thinking about a leaky transmission and suddenly it's three mice playing maracas, these were the cavern walls he had fallen through in one of his dreams when being inducted into the Loup.

All of this was purely secondary. The larger part of Eddie's mind and focus was fixed on the object that all but filled the cavern, the object that they were descending towards. The object that for all the world looked liked a spiked chainmail glove, except about a million times bigger and bristling with enough weapons to turn the eastern seaboard into nothing more than a ketchup stain. The object that was floating in the middle of the chamber as if it had just bitch-slapped gravity and was now enjoying a celebratory drink. The object that Trix Desoto had, somewhat euphemistically, referred to as the Artefact.

As Eddie stared at it, he felt several entire areas of his mind shut down… and several he had never been aware of before, start up.

A number of things, now, became clear – not least being what he had thought was meaningless taunting on the part of Trix on the way down.

The stuff about how there are some people in the world who never bother looking for home, for example – for the simple reason that there is nowhere on this world for them to look.

"Oh God…" he breathed.

"The Artefact," Trix Desoto confirmed. "I tried to clue you in a little, and did I get any credit?"

"Yeah, well you could have done a better job," said Eddie Kalish. "You could have included the single most salient point. That's not a fucking Artefact, that's a fucking Ship."

18.

BUTCHER AND HIS men remained out in the cavern, guarding the elevator platform against the ravening hordes of those who might, for some strange reason, want to spirit it away.

Weirdly enough, you could tell by their postures that each and every one of them was doing his absolute best not to look directly at the Ship.

Eddie Kalish couldn't help noticing, also, that in addition to their heavy armour they had taken up position behind heavy lead shields.

"Look, I'm not trying to be funny or anything—" he began.

"I wouldn't either," said Trix, "the material you've got. This is *funny*, and there you are over on the other side of the room, the material you've got."

"Thank you very much," said Eddie. "You've been a lovely audience and I hope you rot in hell. The thing I was going to say is, how come the soldier-boys get all the neat gear, body armour and shit and we get…" he plucked distastefully at the thin polymer of his coverall "this."

"We don't need anything else," said Trix Desoto. "At least, I don't need anything else and you probably don't. You passed the first test."

"Oh, yeah?" said Eddie. "And what test would that have been, exactly?"

"Here we go," said Trix.

They were at what appeared to be an airlock hatch, a sphincter-like arrangement in the skin of the Ship that seemed every bit as semi-organically repellent, to Eddie, that the word *sphincter* might suggest.

Trix Desoto ran her hand lightly down the… well, down the whatever it was that the skin of the Ship was made of.

"Come on, baby," she murmured. "Open up for me."

Smoothly and silently, the hatch relaxed open.

Eddie gazed dubiously into the darkness beyond.

"I'm not going in there," he said. "There's things in there. Things in the dark. Moving around. I've seen them."

"What are you talking about?" Trix snapped. "What things? Where?"

"Things. Bad things. I've seen them in my head." Eddie had not been entirely serious, of course, but he was still feeling decidedly nervous.

"So we really have to go in there?" he said. "Would it not, I'm saying basically, have been an idea to bring along a couple of flashlights?"

"Don't worry about it," Trix said, climbing up into the hatch. "You coming or not?"

Eddie considered this, for a moment, with some seriousness. Whatever the soldiers were protecting themselves against might be doing horrible things to his body, but he was probably right in assuming that the Loup in Trix and himself was counteracting the effects.

Then again, how much worse might those effects be if you were actually inside the thing that was producing them?

On the other hand, nothing exactly *bad* had happened so far – and how many chances did you get to go inside a genuine alien starship? With the off-chance of coming out with your colon and memoplex intact, in any case.

He realised that he was looking at the outline of Trix against a pale and shifting glow. At least there was light of some kind in

there, in any event. He shrugged to himself and followed her inside.

The tunnels winding through the main mass of the Ship had a tubular and somewhat organic quality, not as if they were crawling through the bowels of some living organism or some such, but like the ship had in some way been grown on organic principles.

Fitful tendrils of electrical activity crackled along the tunnels, clustering in the areas where Trix and Eddie walked. It was as if the Ship itself were attempting to light their way.

"I think she's trying to be helpful," Trix said.

"She?" said Eddie.

"It's just nomenclature," said Trix. "I don't mean anything by it."

"Well I've gotta tell you," said Eddie, "that I can't imagine thinking of this thing as anything other than an *it*."

"Suit yourself," said Trix Desoto. "Now, I've been here before, so we're not going on the grand tour. We just need to find what we're calling a node… and speak of the devil. There we go."

The so-called node was little more than a place where some of the smaller tubes, running through the main tube of the passageway in a manner no doubt analogous to cables or ducts, clustered and fused together in a malformed lump. The electrical activity within it glowed in a way that, while still faint, was markedly brighter than in the tunnel itself.

"These are basically the equivalent of control panels, I think," said Trix. "Put your hand on it."

"What?" said Eddie.

"Put your hand on it. See what happens."

Later, Eddie would think of any number of reasons why just slapping your hand on some unknown piece of alien technology might be a bad idea. At the time, none of them occurred to him. He just did it. It must have been Trix Desoto's tone of voice.

The panel ignited with a blaze of white light. Electrical fire crawled up Eddie's arm and squirrel-caged around his head. His eyes rolled up in his head and the whites glowed, cutting beams through the darkness of the passageway. Flame in the dark.

Eddie snatched his hand away. The electrical activity dissipated instantly, leaving him pale and shaking.

"That's the biggie," Trix Desoto was saying happily. "That's the test. You made basic contact and survived with at least some of your neurones intact." She looked at him, slightly concerned. "How do you feel?"

It was a few seconds before Eddie pulled himself together to the point of being capable of speech.

"It's like it… it's like she *knew* me," he managed at last through chattering teeth. "Like she's been waiting. Waiting so long and… oh, she's *hungry*… she wants food. In her *mouth* she… oh God!"

Abruptly, as though galvanised, he lunged for Trix and grabbed her, pinioning her upper arms. For a moment Trix was startled enough that setting loose the processes of the Loup – processes that might have turned a firmly Leashed Eddie Kalish into the general consistency of guacamole – never occurred to her.

"You've been here before," Eddie rasped, glaring into Trix Desoto's eyes with such ferocity that, for an instant, they seemed to glow every bit as much as when he had laid his hand upon the Node. "You've talked to this thing. You know what she… what it wants to do…"

"Well, uh, yeah, of course," said Trix. "I know what we, that is GenTech, have to do to –"

"Then tell me what the *fuck* is really going on!" Eddie thundered. "You've been screwing me around from up to down, and now you want me to, you want me to be involved in… I want a proper explanation and I want it now!"

"Now you'll remember," said the Talking Head that was currently assuming the persona of Masterton, "*because I must have said it before – I'm sure of it, in fact – that we keep coming back to the same situation over and over again?*"

"You – that is, the real you – might have mentioned something," said Eddie Kalish, "to that effect. You know, in odd moments."

"*Well, quite,*" said the Talking Head. "*And one of those situations is that you come out and say something, and I tell you not to be*

a particular thing. Can you remember what it is, that particular thing?"

"I remember," said Eddie Kalish.

"And what would that particular thing be?"

"A fucking tool," said Eddie Kalish. "All right?"

"A fucking, as you so rightly say, tool," said the Talking Head.

The Talking Head was, basically, a lump of mimetic biogel, hooked up to the Brain Train's command centre systems and imprinted with the memory engrams of Masterton.

Trix had told him that, while he was talking to the Head, she was going to be implementing a lockdown procedure for the entire Base. In a secure situation such as this, with no communications traffic going in or coming out, it was sometimes useful to confer with a player from the outside.

The Talking Head was capable of giving a clear approximation of what Masterton himself might think and say in any given circumstance – and if circumstances happened to fall outside of its parameters it would say so, allowing one to determine if it was worth breaking communications silence and talking to the man himself.

Eddie had decided, for any number of reasons, that he'd leave talking to the man himself as an absolute last resort.

"There's no way you're any kind of fucking alien, or descended from aliens," the Talking Head was saying. *"Not in any sense you're capable of understanding the word* alien, *in any case. That would be completely and utterly ridiculous."*

The Head formed its biogel mouth into a grimace of irritation. *"The word itself has a bad rep these days, what with being appropriated to fuck and back by sad Abductee-Syndrome fuckos sleeping too close to an electrical outlet, and think that every tick they ever get off their dog is a fucking implant.*

"If it'll make you any happier – and fuck knows, that seems to be my function in life at the moment – think of it in terms of Otherness with a capital O. Contact with the Other."

"Other?" Eddie Kalish said. "Other than what?"

"Other than whatever you got, fucko," said the Talking Head. *"Tyre irons, butch-wax, precooked individually wrapped sausages,*

hockey pucks, cellular phones, string, Danish pastries, sousaphones,
hydrogen fusion reactors, the complete works of the Marquis de Sade,
submarines, small trees, dogshit, what the fuck you want? Lemons,
printed circuits, soap, novelty key chains…"

It occurred to Eddie that, through the slightly limited and
simplified responses of the Head, he had just learned something about the character of Masterton the man.

He had listened to the Head converse with a technician or
some such, and the conversation had been purely technical,
without a trace of antagonism or extraneousness. Now the
Head seemed to have fallen into the persona of Eddie Kalish,
himself, as Masterton the man seemed to do when they actually talked. Masterton the man, he realised, had something of
the mimetic about him.

The Loup took this opportunity to take a little bit of information from a pocket and dropped it into his conscious mind:

Pacing and leading, it was called. The operator falls into the
physical and verbal rhythms of the subject, reinforces them by
the repetition of key words and gestures, the glib recitals of
lists – and then takes the subject off in a direction that he, the
operator, wants. Just the sort of semi-hypnotic managerial shit
that a managerial shit like Masterton would have down pat –
only filtered through the somewhat cruder mechanics of the
Head it became that much more jarring and noticeable.

Eddie wondered if the almost constant swearing – from
both the Talking Head and Masterton himself – when in conversation with him was just an exaggeration for the sake of
imitation, or a true representation of how he, Eddie, really
spoke. Pain in the ass if the latter were so, but then again you
could never tell with something like that.

"… *trapeze artists,"* the Head was saying, *"Stilton cheese, grommet-*
bearings, tapas, gingham, loudhailers, Billie Holliday platters, loam…"

Eddie glanced to one of the technicians who ran the Command Module. "Is there a reset button on this? I think it's gone
into a loop or something."

"Hands off, fucko," said the Talking Head. *"I haven't crashed or*
anything. I can just do that shit for longer than is humanly possible."

"So you're, uh, aware of the basic nature of your existence, then?" said Eddie.

"*Course I am,*" said the Head. "*I'm not a complete fucking moron, and it's more than I can say about you.*"

"What," said Eddie, "that I don't know the basic nature of my existence, or I'm a complete moron?"

"*Look into the dead flat marbles that are my eyes,*" said the Head. "*What are the fucking odds. What do you know about Butts?*"

"Do you know," Eddie snapped. "These last few months, seems as like every sucker and his pooch has some snide little thing to say about me and sex. I've got a Testostorossa who thinks I should be mincing around in a pink tutu, Trix Desoto just assumes I like boys as a matter of course and now some glob of solidified goo in the shape of a disembodied head is coming it with the goddamn butts!

"Well, I'm getting sick of it – so let me lay it out once and for all, and you can tell any asshole who asks. I've done it maybe four times in my life, with backroom girls, when I've managed to scrape together the coin. I've got nothing so against the back-room *boys* that I'd run a mile, but then again I don't feel any real need to go across the street. I've no idea what I want out of the rest of my life, you know, if I happen to meet someone, and maybe that's because of this Alienation Syndrome Trix was talk-ing about – but maybe, just maybe, it's because I'm only fucking seventeen years old! So get off my fucking *back*, okay?"

There was a pause.

"*That must have been building up for quite a while there,*" said the Talking Head.

"I suppose," said Eddie.

"*Feel better for getting it off your chest?*" said the Talking Head.

"I suppose," said Eddie.

"*Well, cathartic as all that might be, in a Reichian sort of way,*" said the Talking Head. "*I was actually talking about the author, Oscar Butts.*"

"Oh," said Eddie.

"*Two-bit crime writer who had a lot of stuff published in rags like* Spicy· Detective *either side of the Second World War. I'm surprised*

*you didn't get a complete bio and bibliography along with the Loup,
since the knowledge might have been of actual use."*

"Yeah, well I got stuff about the Romantic Movement that
would blow your socks off," said Eddie. "As they all did to
each other on a regular basis, by all accounts."

"In any event," said the Talking Head, *"Butts's stock in trade
was definite C-grade detective fiction. The kind of story where roscoes
belched and people flung woo. The guy was going nowhere fast, so his
getting drafted and sent to fight in Europe in '42 was no great loss to
literature. But something happened to him in Europe, something that
would change the direction of his future writings.*

*"Nobody's quite sure what that something was. Some people say
it was because he was in the same unit as Henry Kuttner and the
horror writer did a complete number on Butts. He introduced him to
the Cthulhu Mythos — you know, the stuff that Lovecraft, Derleth,
Ashton-Smith and guys like that used to write — and it coloured his
fiction for the rest of his life.*

*"Other people say that his unit were ordered to guard an artefact
that the Nazis were caught trying to smuggle from North Africa
through Italy and the experience drove him mad. Depending on who
you listened to, this artefact was anything from the Spear of Destiny
to a fully operational inter-planetary craft complete with alien corpses.
Sound familiar?*

*"Either way, as soon as he got back stateside he began writing
again. Not the sub-Dashiell Hammett crap he churned out before the
war, but genre-splicing innovative fiction where private dicks were just
as likely to go insane staring at the visage of Tsathoggua as they were
to solve the case and get the girl. Magazines and publishers started to
take note of Butts and his work and it wasn't long before his novels
started to be published. The first was* The Lady From Beyond the
Stars *and that was swiftly followed by* The Killer had a Million
Faces, Murderphillia, The Star Goat—

"Hang on," said Eddie. "You mean like 'Attack of the
Mutant Star Goat' – no tin can is safe? Did it have a big straw
hat on?"

"At the time," said the Head, *"people found his tales quite terrifying. The stories haunted them. The most horrific things they'd ever read."*

"Doesn't sound all that terrifying to me," said Eddie.

"*Well, other times and other sensibilities,*" said the Head. "*Of course, the main reason was that, as a writer, Butts was frankly just a little bit rotten. He tended to cop out of actually describing his entities, ending the story with the narrator delirious, or writing that they're coming for me with their aarg aarg aargh. That left a hole for people to fill with their own worst nightmares. Like looking at a dark reflector. Stick one finger in the pool, there's three fingers pointing back at you, you know?*

"*Of course, you can't get away with ambiguity much these days,*" the Head continued. "*Suckers who can even read, after a fashion, can only follow something simple and point-to-point. Nobody has the nuts for inference in fiction, these days. There's quite enough of that in real life. They need things all spelled out when they read books.*"

"And that's why Butts is important?" said Eddie. He wondered if he was still, somehow, totally failing to grasp the point.

"*It's important as a model for humans dealing with the Other,*" said the Head. "*I mean, ninety per cent of our universe is made up of Dark Matter, which is basically stuff just hanging around – but the name itself makes it sound a bit dangerous and mysterious. Dark Matter, you know?*

"*However discontinuous, however dislocated the Other might be from human experience and terms, those terms are still the only things that count. We eat what we bring to the table, no more, no less.*"

"So what you're telling me, basically," said Eddie, "is that it doesn't matter a damn what's really going on because humans are screwing around with it, and it's only the human screwing around that counts."

"*If I could nod all sagely and smugly I would,*" said the Head. "*As it is I'll just settle for a somewhat smug 'precisely'. Listen up, sport, and I'll clue you in on all the human-level poop.*"

"And it'll finally be the complete and actual truth?" Eddie asked.

"*True as anything else,*" said the Head. "*Sure, why not. Are you sitting comfortably? Then I'll begin…*"

19.

IN THE BOTTOM drawer of the desk was a barely half-finished quart of Wild Turkey, and Colonel Roland Grist could hear it calling to him. It was the proper twenty-five year-old article as well, turn of the century, no dicking around.

He wasn't going to reach for it, though, not with this… well, let's be honest, here, this jumped-up *whore* watching him with her mocking eyes.

Grist found himself longing for the days when life had been simple, the days when he'd seen the world and killed people as an airborne ranger. Afghanistan, Iraq, Iran, Yemen, Syria, Sudan, Zimbabwe. Even twenty years after a bunch of fundamentalist ragheads had flown a few planes into innocent buildings it could still be used as justification for invading hostile nations. God bless America. And if you happen to blind or cripple a few stone-throwing children or make some Congolese girl do something she doesn't want to do on one of these extended vactions then whose to argue? Say what you like, an officer in the US Army still got you some goddamn respect.

Grist couldn't imagine this Desoto girl being made to do a single thing she didn't want. Quite the reverse, in fact.

In fact, Grist had the distinct impression that, should she ever feel like it, she was perfectly capable of spending months of research to find the single worst thing that he would rather stick a gun in his mouth rather than do, just so's she could force him to do it.

"Where's your friend?" Grist asked, more or less for the sake of something to say, and break the contemptuous silence with which she was currently regarding him.

"Eddie's off getting some Head." The Desoto woman shrugged. "I wouldn't worry about it. He's just funny that way."

Her manner became more businesslike.

"The operation's a go," she said. "I want you to lock the base. Total embargo on communications: nothing coming in, nothing going out, you get me?"

It wasn't even an order. It was a flat statement of how the world was going to be.

Nevertheless, Grist felt he ought to stick up for the autonomy of the US Military from commercial concerns.

"That might be, uh, problematic," he said. "We maintain first-strike capability here. We have to maintain constant contact with the Pentagon, with the White House. I can't simply—"

The Desoto woman snorted. "The White House doesn't know you exist and the Pentagon doesn't care. You can try them, if you like, before you lock this place down, but do you know what they're gonna tell you to do? They're gonna tell you to shut up and do exactly what I say because they're picking up the check for this little operation."

The Wild Turkey was really calling now. For an instant, Grist was struck by the vision of racking back the drawer, hauling out the bottle by the neck and smashing it against the side of the Desoto girl's head.

The vision was so profoundly strong that, a second later, Grist realised that he was still sitting there, staring somewhat dumbly at a miraculously reconstituted and unbloodied Trix Desoto.

He even had to make a quick scan for a general lack of broken glass and a closed desk drawer, just to be sure.

He realised that the Desoto girl had spoken and was looking at him, coldly, for an answer.

"I, uh, beg you pardon?" he managed at last. "Ma'am."

"I was merely saying," the Desoto girl said, "that you'd better get used to the fact that you're currently not a lot more than a cloakroom attendant for GenTech, looking after our crap. Now we're handing in the ticket and we want it back."

It HAPPENED BACK in the last century (said the Talking Head), back in the early 1960s and the classified fusion-bomb tests out here in Nevada.

Fusion, as we all know, doesn't produce gamma or particle-radiation fallout, it just makes a fucking great hole in the ground. So it was with some surprise, and not without a certain degree of trepidation, that those involved subsequently detected massive amounts of radioactivity emanating from the impact-crater.

It wasn't *radioactivity*, of course, not in any actual sense we know. It just tripped the Geigers in more or less the same way that radioactivity would.

It exhibited wave-particle properties similar to those of X-rays, or for that matter photons, but there were marked dissimilarities… What do I look like, some science-lecturer guy?

There's reams of waveform analysis and whatever in the files, but the upshot is that there's simply nothing to compare it *to*. It's dissimilar to everything else in the world we know, in certain fundamental respects, and only similar to itself.

The phenomenon was ultimately termed Upsilonic Radiation (the Head continued) and people have spent lives and careers – their own and others – attempting to determine its basic nature and effect.

That's secondary, though. The important thing is that, when they finally managed to knock up suits capable of protecting humans, well enough and long enough, to survive in the test-bomb crater, they found that the detonation had breached what

was obviously an artificial chamber containing what we call the Artefact.

Bit of a suspicious coincidence, that, you say? Well, for one thing, there were one hell of a lot of bomb tests in the Fifties and Sixties, so you might say that we were due. If there was something hanging around down there and waiting to be found.

But more importantly you're talking about what we'll call a false congruity, a confusion between cause and effect. The only reason that we're here to talk about the confluence of events – any confluence of events, for that matter – is that they happened in the first place.

You might was well say: isn't it lucky trousers have two legs, otherwise they wouldn't fit. Isn't it lucky we have all these dogs to eat all the dog-food people make. When people actually had dogs as pets and didn't eat them, anyway. Sometimes shit just happens, basically, to make a profoundly original philosophical point, and you simply have to deal with it.

As for the Artefact itself. You say it's obviously a Ship, and that's good. Very good, in fact. That's the whole point of what we… well, we'll get to that later.

The thing about that is that the first investigators on the scene didn't see a Ship of any kind at all.

They saw any number of things, from a churning glob of protoplasm, to an insanely complicated mass of clockwork, to the Living Christ nailed to the cross, somehow transported through time and actually there. A giant telephone wrapped in barbed wire. Someone's fat ugly mother dead and lying in state. A set of animated nest-tables dancing to "La Cucaracha" but not actually doing it…

It was different for everyone, what they saw – save for those who for some reason simply didn't see a thing at all, and who went into spontaneous psychopathic fits when others insisted that there was, indeed, something there.

Film footage and, later, video, had the same general effect; nobody could agree on what they were seeing. Digital photography, on the other hand, interestingly enough, just shows a haze of dead pixels to everyone.

The Artefact was, simply, Other. It came from Somewhere Else. Some place where human words and concepts simply don't apply. And the upshot was, of course, that the US Government found itself in sole possession of something supremely powerful and unique… with not the slightest idea of what it was.

So they decided to damn well find out.

Disinformation operations were set up, more or less along the lines of Roswell and the like to keep those who might be drawn towards the whole idea of "aliens" the hell out of the way.

Samples were taken, by way of the discovery that… well, samples were taken, anyway. Study of those samples led to quantum jumps in any number of fields, from the processes informing the Rapture Bug field-test in Des Moines and the subsequent Zarathustra procedures, to AI-grade transputer technology, to the containment fields that made hydrogen fusion in vehicles a practicality. The basis for our world, in fact, such as it is.

All very nice, if that's the sort of thing that floats your boat… but none of it led to a breath of understanding as to what the Artefact actually *was*.

A partial breakthrough came just after the turn of the century, when a programme was instituted of exposing live subjects to minute traces of Artefact material.

This was while the US Government was engaged in what was called a War on Terror. Complete and utter nonsense, of course; you might was well declare a War on Literacy – which they were also doing, believe you me; they just didn't come right out and say it.

Anyhow. The thing about waging a war on a *methodology*, as opposed to anything concrete, was that you could target anyone who you pretty much liked, and pretty much get away with anything in the name of it.

Initially, the live subjects were suspected so-called "terrorists", who at the time were busily being detained and stockpiled without due process. The experiments were… not

a success, unless you count spontaneous mutation into something abominable, feculent and dead to be successful.

It was believed that the material itself was in some way attempting to adapt those to whom it was exposed, so they could survive the exposure, and spectacularly failing.

The theory was then advanced that, since the experimental subjects were mostly adults, the altered *genome* was fighting against an already established *phoneme* to catastrophic effect. It was suggested that the procedure be tried using infants.

I know, I know, but remember that the US was fighting, so it said, monsters who would cheerfully murder American babies – and if the cost of fighting them was to do likewise then what were the odds?

In any case, once the idea was mentioned, some bright spark remembered some research that had been done more than twenty years before, in that previous period of venal Republican numbskullery, the 1980s.

The precise same experiments, it transpired, had been conducted under something called the Janus Project, under the aegis of a Secret Service offshoot calling itself Section Eight. And yeah, but of course, didn't that lead to a lot of bureaucratic confusion. Intentionally so. It kept the Project buried under disinformation.

The Janus Project had been reckoned to be a failure, too. The subjects either spontaneously mutated into monstrous et cetera, or absolutely nothing seemed to happen to them at all. Those who survived were dispersed in a manner that wouldn't arouse undue attention, as opposed to merely killing them, and the Project was quietly wrapped up.

Twenty years later, when they went through the files and tracked down the survivors, the government found a small surprise. The science of genetics had advanced more than somewhat – and they found some really freaky things happening with the survivors' junk DNA. And the interesting thing about that was that it was generational. The survivors had passed the modifications on to their kids.

So, of course, there was nothing for it but to haul that second generation of kids in and start the whole procedure of exposing them all over again.

The problem was that, once again, the Project failed. Oh, fewer of the kids actually died, but nothing much else happened either. The Government gave up, dumped people like you out in various out-of-the-way shitholes, decided to go back to being a glorified gun-runner and washed its hands of the whole sorry business.

So, basically, after all that work and effort, all that suffering, the whole thing just turned out to be totally without meaning and pointless. Oh, well. You gotta laugh, eh?

20.

THE COMMUNICATIONS LOCKDOWN of Arbitrary Base did not, of course, extend to official GenTech traffic. In his spartan quarters in the San Angeles Factory, Masterton was now in the process of conversing with Trix Desoto via secured and scrambled satellite phone.

"So you put our Mister Kalish together with the Talking Head?" he asked.

"Yeah," said Trix Desoto. "He was getting somewhat vehement. Seemed like the best thing to do at the time."

"Well, I'm just thanking Christ that I remembered to seriously downgrade its access and capacity," said Masterton. "He should get enough of the truth to satisfy his curiosity, give him some idea of the actual state of play on top if he's lucky and asks the right questions — but it wouldn't do for him to learn... *absolutely* everything, now, would it?"

"If you're talking about what I think you're talking about, then no," said Trix Desoto on the other end of the line. "You'd have no hold on him whatsoever if he happened to learn that particular little titbit. I think it's safe to say that Eddie learning that particular little titbit would end up very bad for you indeed."

"Why, do my ears deceive me, Trix," said Masterton, "or do I hear a note of cunning speculation in your voice?"

"I'm just saying that I know for a fact that there's some stuff you're not telling even me," said Trix Desoto. "You've got my loyalty in this – but don't forget that I've got what Eddie's got. We're not like… basic humans, and you're basically human, and I know the sort of deviousness that basic humans get up to. The games within games you like to play.

"I'm telling you, Masterton, that if you try to pull any of that shit with us, then Eddie Kalish learning an interesting little particular titbit is going to be the least of your worries."

After Trix Desoto had cut the connection, Masterton just sat there for a while, doing and thinking nothing in particular. Then he raised his hands to his black wraparound shades and pulled them from his head.

The shades were inset with remote-feed microcams, hooked to an implant in his visual centre.

Masterton turned the shades around and used them to examine the strange new growths taken root and growing in the involuted ruins of what had once been his eyes.

"Basic human…" he mused to himself. "Ah, Trix, Trix, if you only knew."

FOR WHAT SEEMED to be a long time, Eddie just stood there looking at the Talking Head.

"And that's it, is it?" he said at last. "That's all there is?"

"*You got your special secret origin,*" said the Talking Head, "*plus an explanation for why you don't quite seem to fit into the world. Why you have problems relating to other human beings on even the most basic level. What more do you fucking want?*"

"Well for one thing," said Eddie. "You've just gone out of your way to tell me what happened to me as a kid and then pull the rug out from under me and tell me it's totally meaningless.

"You and – well, *you* – never seem to lose an opportunity to tell me how insignificant I am in the greater scheme of things, how I'm basically nothing but an ambulatory tool…

but that's not strictly true is it? There's something more that you're still not telling me."

"*Do you realise,*" said the Talking Head, "*that you managed to get through that entire little speech without saying the word 'fuck' once? I have to admit that I'm rather impressed.*"

"Fuck being rather impressed!" Eddie shouted. "Stop trying to deflect the question and answer! Tool I might be, but I've got a function that for some reason is incredibly valuable to you and GenTech – and you're gonna fucking well tell me what the fuck it is!"

"*Well, if you're going to be like that,*" said the Head, "*then I'm telling you, yet again, that you simply don't Need to Know. All you need to know is how to do what we tell you, when we tell you. We have… ways of teaching you, if you can't get that little fact through your head.*"

"Oh yes?" said Eddie, softly. "I'd like to see you try."

(It would be later, looking back, that he would realise that this was the point that several technicians in the Command Module started backing away from him in startled alarm. Pressing themselves against the walls in the cold fear of prey finding some predator suddenly dropped into the middle of their enclosure. Replaying the scene, mnemonically, he would recall image-flashes of the muscles of his arms visibly swelling and bulking, his hands elongating into claws. At the time, he simply didn't notice.)

"Let me guess how that might work," Eddie continued, all unaware that his voice was roughening into a snarl. "You threaten to overdose me with the Leash to the point where I simply can't flip out whatsoever happens, then shoot me in the head if I don't follow orders. I suspect that either way – and whether you shoot me in the head or not – that would mess up whatever it is you want me for."

"*Shooting you in the head would definitely end your usefulness,*" said the Talking Head, "*For a while, at any rate, I admit. There are other means that might be brought to bear to ensure your compliance and keep you useful, however.*"

"To the point where, if I was absolutely and persistently determined to screw up whatever it was you want me to do, you'd be able to stop me every single time?"

"*Can this be the itinerate and inveterate fuckaround who we've come to know and love speaking?*" said the Head. "*You don't have persistence and determination in you, boy.*"

There was a slightly odd set to the Talking Head's synthetic features, Eddie thought, but he couldn't quite work out what it was.

It would only be later that he pegged it: somebody who was well aware of the effect a foot-long talon might have on a lump of relatively fragile biogel – and who was doing their very best not to bring the matter up.

"Do you want to try me?" Eddie said. "Just tell me, okay? And I'd be grateful if you stopped ripping the piss out of me and the way I talk while you do it."

For a few moments the talking head was silent. Then:

"*I'd do a little exasperated sigh, at this point,*" it said, "*if I had the lungs.*

"*All right, already. Okay. I'll let you in on one of the somewhat larger secrets, if it'll stop the pissing and moaning and get you at least halfway back in line…*"

21.

It was twenty-four hours later.

Eddie, for his part, was finding his time-sense becoming uncomfortably acute in that respect. The way that something inside him now incremented the passage of time in multiples of twelve. There was something about having the day bisected by the twelve-hourly shots of the Leash that gigged in him.

There were any number of people in the world, he supposed, people with straight jobs in the Multicorps, say, who lived their lives to a regimen of getting up at a certain time, eating at fixed other times, doing some one particular thing for hours on end… but until he had got mixed up with Gen-Tech he'd had nothing in common with the sorry jerks living drone-lives like that. Whatever else he had been through and done, he had never done that.

It was an imposition. The simple fact of living to a schedule not his own. And if he ever got himself into the position of, what, finding himself with a lifetime supply of the Leash and with nobody to dole it out in return for a favour of any kind, wouldn't that just simply mean that GenTech had in a certain sense won after all? They'd have left their mark on him – and

would be leaving needle-marks on him for the rest of his goddamn life.

Over twenty-four hours the chamber under Shed Seven
containing the Artefact – or the Ship, or, apparently, Eddie had
recently learned, the *Hammer of God* – had changed markedly.
The butterfly wing blast hatches in the main elevator shaft had
been retracted and locked back; cables snaked down from the
Brain Train Command rig and hooked to servomanipulators.

The elevator platform itself had been disabled, meaning that
human access to the chamber of the Artefact was now limited
to the emergency maintenance shafts off to one side.

The canisters containing the Brain Train's cargo were now
being lowered down the elevator shaft by way of what was
basically an automated bucket-chain. Then the manipulators
took them and cracked open the canisters. Then a collection
of other, specialised mechanisms took care of the rather more
horribly organic containers thus revealed.

"It's an old pathologist's joke, apparently," said Trix Desoto.
"The human brain is a remarkably delicate and slippery little
customer to deal with. Fortunately it comes in a padded case.
With handles."

She didn't seem one bit distressed at all the busy servome-
chanical activity as the heads were shelled and discarded in
untidy piled, their contents slopped onto conveyor-belts that
trundled them off, through an intake hatch, into the dark
bowels of the Ship. She just stood there, relaxed, the case she
had brought from the Command rig hanging from her hand.

The case was of around the same size and construction as
might be suitable for carrying a snare drum around, built from
rib-reinforced aluminium with polycarbon impact-pads.

Eddie had an idea of what might be in it. All the clues were
there. He shuddered, and recalled what the Talking Head with
the persona of Masterton had finally told him.

Now THE THING you have to bear in mind (said the Talking
Head) is that almost everything you think you know, everything you've been told so far, is basically a lie.

Oh, do stop growling at me like that. It's not impressing anyone. What you've been told is technically factual, so far as such things can be known, given that we're dealing with things that nobody sees the same way and everyone has a different opinion about. You've been told the truth, just not all if it – which is, of course, the very best kind of lie there is.

The lie, er, lies in the ambiguous nature of the Artefact itself. The fact that in a certain sense it lies outside the bounds of human comprehension has given the impression that the very *issues* that surround it lie outside the bounds of human comprehension. This isn't actually so. The issues themselves are really quite simple. Ridiculously so, in fact. You'll laugh when I tell you. Oh, go on.

The fact is that there are many… well, let's call them Factions in this world. And, whoops, that's a tricky one right from the start. Let's just say that by *world* we mean, you know, maybe it's not just this world and leave it at that, all right? That's not the point.

The point is that these Factions are real. Now, it's not like you can categorise them as Light and Dark – while remembering that "light" doesn't necessarily mean *good* any more than "dark" means *evil*. You need to think in terms of team colours for some sport or other. And think of their supporters as being like the soccer fans the Brits have over the pond, who aren't exactly charmers, whichever team they root for.

They've existed as long as man has walked the earth. Even before the early humans learned not to walk with their knuckles scraping the ground, they were forming up into tribes and marking their territory and hunting grounds. Not unlike how things are today, it's just that the hunting grounds have changed somewhat. Instead of an acre of fertile soil, today's territories are the airwaves, the boardrooms, the human spirit, the space between your ears and other less tangible frontiers that you just wouldn't be able to get your head around.

But what is important, and what you can comprehend, is that everything that happens of any importance on this planet is a

direct result of a Faction's influence. If two African nations go to war because one side doesn't like the shade of the other side's skin, it's because one Faction or another made it happen. If a young starlet at the peak of her career is brutally slain in her Beverly Hills mansion, you can bet there's Faction involvement somewhere along the line. And if the Colombian coffee crop fails for three consecutive years then you can stake your house on its cause having something to do with a Faction. It's just the way of the world and it's how it's been for thousands of years.

In any event, the thing we're calling the Artefact was discovered some time during our planet's history by one of these Factions, here in its chamber on Earth. Ever since then it's been guarded and protected, kept in reserve for some grand strategic move or other a couple of thousand years down the line – so far as here and now we reckon time.

But why, and more importantly, how is it here? Is it, as one particular Faction believes, a gift from some ancient alien culture? Or an ancient alien culture in its entirety as another believes?

Or is it, in the end, nothing more nor less difficult and complicated than a Ship? The space-going equivalent of an aircraft carrier, from what I'm told, designated by a name that comes out in the translation as *Hammer of God* or some such.

The reason why it projects such a sense of Otherness, the reason why so many can't see it for what it is, is simply that it's discontinuous with the here and now of our world. It has no place here, no common terms of reference.

Imagine if Neanderthal man were to come across an F1-11 fighter plane that had somehow been dropped in through a hole in space/time. Somebody might learn that if you stick a finger in the electrics, you get a nasty shock. Somebody might accidentally switch on the comms and get an earful of static. That's about the extent of what anyone would learn – and that's the equivalent of what human beings, here and now, have managed to achieve by a process of back-engineering.

The thing about that, though, is that by just generally dicking around, we came to the notice of its owners. Somebody heard us babbling into the radio, as it were.

And so this new Faction made contact. Datanets had nervous breakdowns, the heads of scores of sensitives around the world literally exploding, the whole bit. It was chaos for a while, before the Faction caught on to what was happening and ramped their processes down.

Anyhow. Contact was eventually achieved, and a deal brokered. The new Faction are to get their *Hammer of God* back and we, well we get our hands on some a simplified extraterrestrial craft that we can actually understand and reverse engineer. Just as the technology recovered from the Roswell craft led to the invention of microwave ovens, e-mail and pay-per-view porn, these new discoveries will lead to hundreds more breakthroughs. Teleportation. Time travel. Perpetual motion machines. You name it, we could have it.

And the best thing is that they think we're doing them a favour. They haven't got a clue that we don't know the first thing about how to extract the Artefact's secrets and its very presence here is beginning to throw things way out of kilter. Do you think it's a coincidence that the land for hundreds of miles around here is so dry that even cacti have difficulty growing? So we're going to exchange this unknowable heap of junk for an alien museum piece that was obsolete before Cain even threw Abel a funny look.

To do that, though, they need the damn thing up and running. Maintenance and activation sequences have to be carried out – bit of a tricky thing to do if you happen to be an entity that can't access the world in any truly physical sense without bursting the whole thing like a soap bubble. And doubly problematic if you then have to rely on a bunch of overgrown monkeys who see the thing as any and all manner of other weird things, if they can even see it at all.

The solution, in the end, was to engineer some overgrown monkeys who could see the thing for what it was – and this is where the operation directly concerns you. A routine gene-examination of your body, after you got yourself shot up in New Mexico, threw up a whole bunch of flags.

There are standing orders to bring in anyone showing signs of being legacy offspring from the old Janus Programmes, because the modifications to their junk DNA already put them halfway down the road. There was only an off-chance possibility that you might be viable, but the opportunity was too good to miss. That's why we patched you up.

The Faction worked with GenTech in tweaking a whole bunch of back-engineered Zarathustra processes to produce the Loup. We heaved in a lot of other stuff, of course, but the main thing – the *important* thing – is that you can see the *Hammer of God* for what it is and, to some extent, manipulate its systems. Your mind and body have been retuned to have an affinity with it on several quite profoundly fundamental levels.

You're not buying this, are you, Eddie? It's written all over your face. Okay, try this one: what if this new alien Faction isn't a new Faction? What if it's just a different aspect of one of the already existing Factions and it's been fighting against the other Factions out in space? What if it's been fighting them since the dawn of time, is still fighting them now and will, in all likelihood, be fighting them for eternity?

What if this ship isn't here by accident? What if the Faction has been using this planet as storage depot for the last however many years and now they need the Artefact to wage a war a million billion light years away? What if there aren't thousands of different Factions but just four? What if what we think are different Factions are just aspects of these four?

Do you buy that? Well do you, Eddie? Would you give me a dollar for that? No. I didn't think you would.

The upshot is, you took one look at something that drives almost any other human into the bughatch, in any number of ways, and just went, "Oh, yeah, that's a Ship." You got the right stuff, Eddie boy. Congratulations.

Or maybe everything I've just told you has been another huge lie just to keep you off balance and under control. Either way, I wouldn't let it bother you. All that matters in the here and now is that there's a job that needs doing and you're the only person who can do it for us.

Don't get too far up yourself though. In the end you're still not much more than a chimp whose been trained to use a spanner. Now, if we've all finished sucking one another's dicks, let's get to work.

22.

THE TUBULAR PASSAGES running through the Ship were far more brightly lit than the last time Eddie Kalish had been here. Electrical activity crackled and seethed along the walls, which had themselves taken on a glowing and translucent aspect, complicated forms like multicoloured oils mixed with water spiralling lazily within them.

For hours Eddie and Trix Desoto worked their way through the Ship, following a schematic that had been, apparently, downloaded by the Faction into the GenTech datanet in a kind of abreactive cybernetic fit that had cut services to three entire GenTech-owned compound-blocks for a month.

They worked to a step-pattern so that Trix was always working on a node while Eddie worked on another nearby. The work itself, it seemed to Eddie, was remarkably simple; he would simply place his fingers on a node and sense a change in the energy flows within, redirect them by a repositioning of his fingers until he felt inside himself that their configuration was correct. Presumably this knowledge had been implanted on some subconscious level via the Loup.

He was reminded of the time back in the hospital room of the Factory, where he had accessed the datanet without ever quite knowing how he was doing it.

Their tandem path took them through spaces that might or might not have been living-quarters, command centres, chambers that appeared to be armament-depositories or hangars for small craft that were, he supposed, the extraterrestrial equivalent of tactical fighters. All the while, the throbbing sense of power accumulating inside the Ship grew stronger.

This reminded Eddie, despite himself, of what was actually feeding it.

"What's it eating?" he asked Trix. "Neuropeptides or something? And thank you, Mister the Loup, for throwing up the word *neuropeptides* when I don't know what the hell it actually means. What I mean is, if it's eating stuff you find in the brains then why can't GenTech just synthesise it or something?"

"It doesn't work like that," said Trix. "The Ship isn't digesting the… material as nutrients."

The material, Eddie thought. She's acting like she just doesn't care, but she's putting up another front. Like she tried to turn it into a joke before. Why didn't I notice that before?

"The Ship's liquefying and extruding the material," Trix Desoto was saying. "Patching it into her own neurotecture. I gather that she operates by way of an interconnected complex of microtubular filaments, operating on the quantum level, hooking into the very fabric of space/time. Drawing power from the fundamental wave-form resonance of the universe itself.

"We got the model from a basic template that the Faction encoded into a clone-host – that old guy I was transporting when we first met, yeah? The parameters were quite clear. And the only real source for those particular microtubular constructs, here and now on Earth, is the human brain."

"Yeah, but if you got it from a clone-host, whatever the hell that is, then you can clone a–"

"Doesn't work," said Trix Desoto. "A clone we're capable of producing unassisted, under the current state of the art, by its very nature never makes synaptic links or achieves

consciousness. Has to be a brain from someone conscious and alive – or at least who was."

"All the same," Eddie said. "It all still seems a bit–"

"I know what you mean," said Trix. "Fundamental lack of connection with other human beings is one thing, but I still think it's a little bit off."

Eddie couldn't work out for the life of him if she had meant that as a joke or not. It would open up a number of not entirely comforting questions either way.

He realised that Trix Desoto had said something else.

"What?" he asked her. "What did you say?"

"I said that, on the other hand, what's the alternative? The destruction of the universe? Or at least, the destruction of that bit of it with Earth and all the human beings on it?"

Eddie Kalish pondered that for a moment.

"I'm going to ask you what you said again," he said at last. "But, you know, I mean it in a slightly different way."

"We don't get the Ship up and running," said Trix Desoto, "then the Faction who wants it is just going to lean in – from wherever it is they lean from – and simply grab it. You think the world's showing cracks now, just you wait until the *Hammer of God* starts shaking it up like a snow globe. Didn't the Head get around to telling you that?"

"Not as such, no," said Eddie. "And on the whole I'm somewhat glad it didn't."

They continued on through the Ship, reconfiguring the nodes, Trix still lugging whatever it was that was in her case. The corridors branched and interconnected in any number of ways, but they followed the schematics on a rough trajectory spiralling to the centre.

They were getting quite close. It was hot and the Ship was pounding around him and Eddie's skin tingled. He felt muscle-masses shifting around under it. Up ahead, Trix Desoto's form seemed slightly more bulky, her gait more loping.

He hurried forward to catch her up, laid a hand on her shoulder. She swung round, snarling, for a moment her eyes blazing. Then she visibly caught herself.

"I think the Ship's triggering the Loup," he told her, taking a somewhat hurried step back. "Even through the Leash. Maybe I need a booster shot or–"

"An imposed reversion would probably kill you at this point," Trix Desoto said. "It's the other way around. The Loup's cutting in, despite the Leash, this near to the core, to compensate for an increase in upsilonic radiation. My advice is just to go along with it and–"

And it was at this point that the explosive charges detonated outside and things went, even more than usual, totally to hell.

23.

It might have been wondered, by those in a position to wonder, why the various GenTech technicians and operatives were going along with something like the Brain Train. They did not, after all, have the Alienation Syndrome shared by Eddie Kalish and Trix Desoto, and so presumably cared about their fellow human beings and what happened to them – at least so much as human beings generally do.

One reason, of course, was that it is very hard to overestimate what people will do as part of the drudging and day-to-day business of participating in atrocity.

And then there are those who simply have a propensity for cruelty and violence – indeed, the Brain Train's security force, the outriders and those who handled the weapons systems, were of just that sort. Violent men, and for that matter women, who didn't care who they might end up fighting just so long as they fought.

Just the sort of people you needed, in fact, out on the dangerous and somewhat crazy blacktops of America.

As for the technicians themselves, most of them didn't call the Brain Train by that name, and probably didn't even know

it. In the time-honoured commercial tradition of the left hand not knowing what the right was doing, most of them thought that they were delivering components for a new supercomputer-system – components which had to be kept in refrigerated canisters on account of their extreme delicacy.

Those who knew the actual nature of the Brain Train's cargo thought that they were still components for a new supercomputer-system – but they were clone-brains, grown whole in the GenTech skeining vats. One or two might have had their suspicions – in the same way that an employee in a Mister Meaty burger bar might have suspicions as to precisely what goes into the burgers – but not to the point where they might investigate, due to the horrible possibility that their suspicions might be confirmed.

Besides, it wasn't their job. Let someone else get into trouble and take the heat for it if they wanted.

In short, while they might be living under a certain element of corporate-drone denial, the GenTech Brain Train technical crew were not particularly bad or callous people.

As such, it could be argued that they did not deserve what would happen to them when as squad of US troops from the Base approached them, as they were going about their business, brought up their MultiFunction rifles and began to slaughter them out of hand.

For a while it was bloody. Then the Brain Train's own security forces woke up to what was happening, weighed in on the side of GenTech and things got bloodier still.

OUTSIDE, FROM OUTSIDE the Ship, there was a heavy concussion. The ship lurched.

Somewhere in the back of Eddie's head, a gentle murmuring of which he had been barely aware other than that it was vaguely comforting, suddenly became the shriek of fingernails on slate.

It was the Ship, he realised. Up until now the Ship had just been murmuring about how happy it was to be here and alive and waking up – and now it was squealing in alarm.

"That came from outside!" Trix Desoto snapped. "That was an attack! Go and see what's happening."

Eddie Kalish was of the profound opinion that, if something were attacking, the least safest place to be would be outside the protection afforded by a *Hammer of God*.

"What about the activation?" he said. "We can't just–"

"I can take care of the rest of the nodes," Trix Desoto said. "There's only a few left." She hefted the case she was carrying meaningfully. "And plus I'm the only one who knows what to do with the… final component. I'm the only one who can get it done."

"I don't suppose you could give me a quick run down, then?" Eddie asked. "I mean listen, I'm really not trying to be the rat here – all right, who am I kidding, course I'm being a cowardly little rat. But the fact remains that you're the lethal one. You've got the Loup under control. Whatever's out there, you're the one who can flip out and waste it, while I–"

"Trust me, wouldn't work," said Trix Desoto. "There's no time to explain it but just trust me but there's no *way* it would work. I wish to God, quite frankly, that there was someone else who could go out there and watch my back, but you're the only one I've got. Just get out there and *do* it, okay?"

EDDIE KALISH TOOK of the larger tubes and just trusted that it would lead to a sphincter-hatch that would let him out of the Ship.

Some large part of him, of course, hoped that it would just lead to a dead end, giving him the excuse to just blunder about and get confused and not have to go out in the end at all.

In the event, though, the tube led him straight to a hatch in a matter of minutes, bang on order. Just his luck.

He wondered, briefly, if he should stroke the wall in the same way that Trix Desoto had done, but the hatch simply dilated in front of him. He would never be sure if the Ship itself was trying to be helpful – or if it simply wanted to be rid of him.

The air outside was hazed with smoke. Eddie stuck his head out of the hatch, hauled it back and examined the image imprinted on his retinas. Nothing moving out there. Nothing alive.

Cautiously, he clambered down from the hatch, went into a crouch and scanned his surroundings through the haze. Now that he was through the hatch he became of a loud, low rumbling emanating from the Ship itself. Whatever provided its motive force was obviously on line.

The cavern was a mess. The servomechanisms that had been busily shucking human heads were a tangled, burning wreckage – the source of the smoke. There was the smell of charred flesh from the piles of discarded empty heads.

Somebody had dropped a quantity of hi-ex down the main elevator shaft and taken the various head-processing units out. Eddie wondered if the idea had been to disrupt the Ship's replenishment, before remembering that part of the operation had been almost done in any case before he and Trix had entered to reconfigure the nodes. Whoever had done this would have known that, or simply didn't care.

In any case, here and now, there didn't seem to be any immediate threat. He turned back, intending to return to Trix Desoto and tell her as much, and found that the hatch had contracted shut.

Abruptly, the rumbling from the Ship changed in tone, and added several extra harmonics to the mix. Eddie had been around enough vehicles, of various types, in his life to recognise that several key systems had just cut in. The Ship was in the process of prepping for actual flight.

Eddie Kalish had not the slightest idea what might happen to him, should a starship from the future, or the past, or from some weird dimension of wherever the fuck it was, decided to take off in an enclosed space with him standing right beside it – and it was the considered opinion of one Eddie Kalish that he was fucked if he was gonna wait to find out. He scrambled through the wreckage and sloshed and crunched his way through the detritus of shelled and emptied heads to the

alcoves leading to the emergency maintenance shafts – only to find them filled with quick-drying concrete.

The concrete was still vaguely sludgy, but not so much that there would be any possible way through it. When the US Army Engineering Corps start throwing construction materials around, they don't dick about.

Behind him, the rumbling of the Ship cranked up another notch and became a positive roar.

One chance left, then.

The pylons and the cogwheel rack that had respectively stabilised and given purchase for the main elevator platform were a scorched and buckled, collapsed mess, but he was able to haul himself up on them to gain some height.

Hanging from the elevator shaft itself, in the roof of the cavern, was a length of gear-chain that remained from the mechanism that had lowered the canisters of the Brain Train's cargo.

Eddie Kalish launched himself for it desperately, brushed the chain with his outflung fingers and fell back – flat-foot boosted himself against the remains of a crumpled stanchion, managed somehow to get his hand round the chain and then clung on for dear life.

(And it was only later, yet again, that he would work out the various distances and dynamics, and realise that what he had done was physically impossible. He was really going to have to gat a handle on that, he thought later – work out the limits of what his Loup-informed body was really able to do, if only to stop all this waking up in a cold sweat the night after he did stuff.)

Eddie hauled himself up to get a purchase with his other hand, wondering if he really had it in him to make it up the shaft by way of a gear chain that was already slicing into him.

Below him, the roar from the Ship ramped up yet again.

Problem solved. Eddie climbed.

24.

COLONEL ROLAND GRIST sat on the floor in Arbitrary Base Tactical Command, looking down numbly at the liquid seeping numbly out across the carpet from between his legs.

The liquid, it must be said, was actually the better part of a bottle of Wild Turkey, his fourth in the space of twenty-four hours, which had slipped from his fingers, with which he was currently and unaccountably having some degree of trouble.

Oh, well. He had probably had enough by this point anyway. He still had other bottles salted away in his quarters. And the smell of it helped to counteract the smell of the piss.

One step leading to another. Step by logical step. How could things have gotten so far out of hand so fast? How had it all turned into shit?

The Desoto girl humiliating him the day before had been nothing new to Grist; he had, after all spent the best part of a decade in a state of humiliation.

Jealousy amongst the powers that be in the Pentagon, that's what it was. Following his successes in Madagascar back in '09, including the depersonalization and deforestation of the entire island, the powers that be spotted his rising star and decided to

slap it down out of hand. Dishonourable discharge they'd called it, not that Grist could see anything dishonourable in using a little napalm to sort out a problem with local insurgents. How can you make an omelette if you can't break a few eggs?

Following his court martial, the CNG had welcomed him with open arms and allowed him to carry over his army rank of colonel. He had been appointed in Command of Arbitrary Base (Fort Dix, as it was) and its complement of intercontinental ballistic missiles, each capable of wiping out a major city, halfway around the globe in any direction you might like. Half a century before, with actual superpowers standing off under the threat of Mutually Assured Destruction, that might have been a big deal.

The fact was, however, that by the turn of the twenty-first century, the dynamic of global conflict was shifting irrevocably to the smaller scale. Police actions and surgical incursions were the way to go – and in none of these was there any sensible scenario involving the annihilation of entire major cities.

Grist had become, as the Desoto girl had reminded him, nothing more than a glorified caretaker, taking care of stuff until such a time as there might be a need for it again – and when that time came, of course, the stuff would be taken from him. He wouldn't even get a go with the button.

Then again, as if in response to their general insignificance to the world, advances in technology had refined the stopping-power of an ICBM into something that could be carried on the back of a roller skate. And while people are forever saying that it's not the size, it's what you do with it that counts, that's a fucking lie and they know it. When Colonel Grist had contemplated the relative size of his arsenal, it couldn't but have him feeling like a dickless fuck.

And as if to add insult to injury, the jokers had informed him that he was responsible for a subterranean chamber containing what they called the Artefact. Extraterrestrial in origin, they said. Most important thing in the world they said. Second only to the… thing that the Roswell Incident was invented to deflect attention from, they said.

And Grist had believed them. They had seemed so serious about it. Grist had taken up his new post almost bursting with pride… and then gone down the Shed Seven shaft to find nothing but a disused weapons repository. Nothing inside whatsoever. His superiors had been ripping the piss out of him. Laughing at him behind his back.

They were doing that little twirly thing with a finger to the ear, too, in his mind.

Grist had decided, then and there, looking at nothing whatsoever, that he'd be jiggered if he was going to be the one to crack first. For a decade he had played along, each status report on this so-called Artefact adding another little drop of acid to his soul. The only thing that had kept him going was the knowledge that the bastards in the Pentagon knew he knew, and was playing them at their own game, and that it must be driving them completely bugshit.

Evidently, it was working. Now they had stepped up the ante – sending in a bunch of GenTech civilians to rub it in and mock him. Acting as if the so-called Artefact existed and was of supreme importance. Doing it all to mock him and watch him squirm.

There was absolutely no other explanation, given that the so-called Artefact simply didn't exist.

Grist had decided to let them get on with their little farce, and left them to it. Screw 'em, frankly. He was just going to go off and get tanked.

After a day and light of miserable drinking in his quarters, however, something had snapped. He just wasn't going to take it anymore. He could see the way before him clearly.

He had gathered together those of his men who he knew, so far as such things can be known, were not in on the so-called Artefact joke, and informed them that Special Forces Intelligence had reported that these GenTech guys were in fact impostors – here to secure the Arbitrary Base nuclear arsenal in the name of New Congolese Vengeance. He had ordered his men to take them down with all necessary force.

He'd always been good at making stuff up off the top of his head like that, and sending his guys in on the basis if it. It had reminded him of the good old days.

Of course, he could never have anticipated how the Gen-Tech guys responded to an attack. How the hell would a bunch of play-actors and practical jokers be so well trained and armed? There was just no way it made sense.

And then, of course, there were the filthy traitors, who had refused to follow orders. Fortunately, before ordering those he trusted to attack the GenTech team, Grist had contrived to secure those he did not fully trust in their barracks huts, where a number of time-delayed cyanide capsules had taken care of the problem nicely, thank you very much. Problem solved.

Unfortunately, one could not be expected to think of everything.

With the GenTech team fighting back so unexpectedly against his troops, and the Arbitrary Base compound dissolving into chaos, Grist had decided that his proper place was to be here in Tactical Command. He had arrived here, though, to find it guarded by one of his lieutenants, a Lieutenant Butcher, who had promptly attempted to take him into custody. Him!

Then things had gotten just a little bit confused. It was probably the drink. The next thing Grist knew he was sitting here, the entire left side of hs head throbbing with pain, and he was somehow holding Butcher's sidearm.

The body of Butcher lay before him, as it did now, with its head quite comprehensively blown off.

Grist couldn't remember firing the gun even once, let alone enough times as it would take to inflict the damage done to Butcher. He simply had no memory of it. The term "psychotic cleavage" surfaced through his sodden mind. Then he forgot it.

Now Grist staggered to his feet. Something detonated outside. The ground shook. It was time for action, and he was just the guy to take it.

The control panels in Tactical Command gave direct access to the SNARKs off in their silo-racks. That was the stuff to give 'em. Make the damn Congolese pay.

Through a combination of drink, psychosis and concussion sustained during his struggle with Butcher, Colonel Grist had simply forgotten that his hastily-invented lie about the New Congolese Vengeance terrorists was a fabrication. There had been a terrorist attack on US soil and the bastards responsible were going to *pay!*

It occurred to Grist, though, that he might need command-code clearance before proceeding with the launch. Fortunately, Tactical Command had a satellite-hotline overriding any lockdown or communications-blackout procedure.

Grist grabbed the handset. "Get me c-in-c Special Services Operations now," he barked.

"This is Special Services Operations at the Pentagon." A chirpy recorded voice said. *"If you require our humanitarian intervention in a territorial, religious or political dispute, please press one. If you wish to report an alleged atrocity carried out in the name of Uncle Sam by our boys overseas, please press two. For all other services, please hold the line."*

And then the handset, for some reason, began playing the Village People singing 'In the Navy'. Colonel Roland Grist stood to attention, handset to his ear, and waited for it to stop.

EDDIE KALISH HAULED himself from the elevator shaft. The Shed that had enclosed it was gone, at least in terms of being a Shed, having been converted to twisted scraps of metal sheeting spread over quite some area.

The compound of Arbitrary Base, likewise, had been converted to a battlefield devastation of twisted, burning bodies and wreckage. Eddie was reminded of the attempted hijacking of the Road Train, back when he had first met Trix Desoto – but ramped up to the *n*th degree. Military-spec weaponry and tactics versus the enhanced defences and armaments GenTech had brought along for this operation.

The Mobile Command Centre was totalled. Everybody Eddie could see was dead. There were rather less soldiers than he remembered among the corpses – and this gave Eddie Kalish pause for thought. If there were less dead soldiers then

that meant, of course, that there was a better chance of living ones still knocking about.

Eddie made his way through the wreckage, senses alive for any sight or sound of movement or life, ready to cut and run at any moment.

It was a bit depressing, now he came to thing of it, that his life contrived to place him in this precise situation over and over again. He wondered if there was somebody he could complain to about it.

In the end, as it happened, he found a sign of life – but from a different and unexpected direction, and far less welcome than even some surviving Delta Marine with an M37 and an attitude about how many of his friends had been killed would have been. There was a roar overhead and a VTOL descended like the wrath of God – if God had happened to have access to next-generation VTOL technology and was really, really pissed off.

The craft was of a somewhat different design to the Gen-Tech flyer that Eddie had encountered in Little Deke's junk yard, which had transported a squad of operatives who had ended shooting Eddie stone cold dead.

This was not exactly comforting in that it was built on the basis of several streamlined polycarbon helium-pontoons to give it positive lift, and multidirectional turbines that could move it in any direction it liked, and do it fast.

The upshot was that the thing was damn *huge*, and looked like it was the sort of thing that could carry tanks. Stencilled prominently on its underside – in accordance with the convention in what might be called the Corporate Wars that those involved in overt action must tell their immediate opponent just who the hell they are – was the logo:

neogen

"Oh great," said Eddie, looking up at it. "What are the fucking odds?"

25.

THE NEOGEN VTOL banked in the air and, as a matter of first principles, took out Arbitrary Base Tactical Command with a couple of well-aimed Exocets. This was rather more fortunate than otherwise, in the general human scheme of things, since Colonel Roland Grist had at that precise moment grown tired of listening to the Village People singing "In the Navy" and was on the point of launching the SNARKs just for the hell of it.

The Confederated Republics of the Congo would never know how lucky they were – though due to their current problems with an entirely other arm of the US Military, it is doubtful that they would have even noticed.

Now the NeoGen VTOL descended, ejecting what at first sight appeared to be bulky, ape-like forms, each twice the size of an ordinary man. They hit the ground and advanced – not lumbering but at an incongruously brisk double-time pace.

Eddie Kalish, cowering behind the overturned remains of a portable latrine-pod, set up by GenTech the very instant they had seen the military-pristine but military-basic state of the sanitation in Arbitrary Base, stared at these advancing forms…

and the Loup took the opportunity to drop yet another piece of useful information into his head.

"Oh shit…" he muttered to himself. "NeoGen have Faction backing, too."

As if in direct confirmation of his supposition, an amplified voice began to blare from the VTOL:

"HEY, LISTEN UP, YOU GUYS," it blared. "WE REALLY, REALLY, WHEN IT GETS RIGHT DOWN TO IT, DON'T WANNA DO THIS THING WITH ALL THE FUSSIN' AND THE FIGHTIN'. IT'S JUST SO BAD FOR THE KARMA AND IT ALL GETS SO SCREWED UP, YOU KNOW? TELL YOU WHAT, WHY NOT TAKE SOME MELLOW-TIME, GIVE US THE *HAMMER OF GOD* AND THEN WE… GUYS?"

There was the amplified sound of a hand being placed over a microphone and the subdued mumble of conversation. Then:

"HEY, LOOKS LIKE THEY'RE ALL DEAD. HOW THE FUCK DID THAT HAPPEN? AH, WELL, FUCK 'EM. GO AND GET THE THING SECURE, GUYS."

This, presumably, directed at the power-armoured soldiers, who now changed course to head directly to the mouth of the Shed Seven elevator shaft. And, incidentally, almost exactly to the point where one Eddie Kalish was hiding.

Then things went from bad to worse.

TRIX DESOTO LURCHED through the tubes of the Ship, reconfiguring the final nodes.

Electrical activity thrashed and stuttered around her, racking up by increments with every Node she passed. The pulsing roar of the Ship around her acquired harmonic after harmonic, until in the end it seemed like nothing more nor less than white noise – every audible frequency was filled, in the same way that a cough can momentarily drown out every other voice in a crowded room.

She had long since lost the clean-room polymer coveralls, and for that matter all but a scrap of the clothing beneath. The Loup inside her was desperately attempting to compensate for

the increased activity of the Ship. It constantly formed and reformed her, so that one second she might look like nothing more than a naked and extremely well-muscled girl, the next a twisted, hulking horror.

As she approached the Core, the frequency and severity of the transitions increased, to the point where the flesh of her body seemed to haze around her bones.

Now, at last, she stood before the Core.

Disappointingly enough, it was not exactly impressive. It was simply a hole in the world. An obloidular portal, hanging in the air, leading to… not blackness, but absolute nothingness. A void waiting to be filled.

A mouth waiting to be fed.

The malformed hazing mouth of Trix Desoto attempted to form words. "Brought you something," she managed in a guttural slur. "Brought you something nice. Something nice for your mouth."

She attempted to open the case she held. In her transforming and retransforming state, she had a bit of trouble with the catches, and ended up having to literally tear it open.

Inside was a customised and somewhat complicated piece of medical equipment: a number of articulated blades and hooks controlled by way of a pair of handles. It was, basically, a rib-spreader so contrived that the user could operate upon his or herself.

And this is what Trix Desoto proceeded to do.

Or, at least, this is what she attempted to do. The blades of the spreader hit her Loup-transforming chest and shattered.

"Shit," said Trix Desoto.

UP IN THE Arbitrary Base compound, Eddie Kalish was sharing a similar sentiment, although the language was somewhat more extreme.

"Fuck me backwards…" he muttered as the armoured NeoGen troops advanced. It could only be a matter of seconds before one of them spotted him, racked out his big Multi-Function Gun and blew his head off.

Possibly, he should have thought to liberate a weapon from the GenTech team or a dead US trooper. Not that it would have done the slightest good, of course. It would just have been nice to have an actual prop when he went, "Look, I'm dropping my weapon, please don't kill me!"

Eddie Kalish decided that, at this point, he had two choices:

1) He could stay exactly where he was and wait for some power-armoured NeoGen trooper to spot him, when he was almost certainly going to be automatically shot on sight.

Or:

2) He could make his presence known, and hope that a generally weaselly but inoffensive demeanour might keep him alive long enough to actually surrender. If they didn't just automatically shoot him on sight.

While the first option had the advantage that he didn't have to do anything about it, Eddie decided that, on the whole, the second might be the safer option. Moving as slowly and unthreateningly as he could, he clambered out from behind the latrine pot and stuck his empty hands in the air.

"Hey guys?" he called. "I'm… uh… a non-combatant, here! Is there, like any way we can—"

Automatic fire stitched into the ground before him, and Eddie dived back behind the latrine pod. Oh, well. It had been a long shot at best. The only thing for it, he supposed, was to go about preparing himself for death.

He wondered how you were supposed to go about the business of doing something like that. The number of times he'd had to do that lately, in his life, he really should have gotten around to asking someone. Maybe there was a pamphlet or something.

In any case, judging by the radio-static garbled orders now being barked to the advancing NeoGen troops, it didn't make any odds. Death was coming, and coming now, whether Eddie Kalish was prepared for it or not.

IN THE CORE of the Ship, Trix Desoto dropped the surgical device and swore an oath so vile that it, if she were Catholic, would have her saying Hail Marys until the end of time.

She stood there for a moment, gazing into the hole of the Core with burning eyes, her transmuting flesh seething and sliding around her bones.

Then she took one clawlike hand, and plunged it into her chest. Clenched the talons around what it found there and wrenched it out.

There was surprisingly little blood. The explosion of fluid seemed to be more plasmic in nature – plasma such as you would find on the burning surface of a star.

The thing she now held, in what once had been her hand, might have once been, on the crude and merely physical level, her heart.

Transformed, now, folding into itself at some direction from a right-angle to reality and constantly changing form. Now an abstract representation, like the cartoon-love heart one might find on a particularly saccharine and sickly Valentines' card.

Now a homunculus – a little thing not shaped precisely like a human being, but capturing in its form every abstract aspect of what a human being was.

Now a glowing sigil that would be meaningless to any and every other human being on the planet – the sign of the secret, sacred and unique name that is carved on the heart of every living and self-aware thing…

Trix Desoto held her burning heart up to the Core.

"For you," she said, perfectly calm and lucid despite her Loup-transforming state. "For your mouth."

With the last of her strength, she plunged the heart into the Core.

An explosion of energies and activity that made all those previous pale by comparison. The chamber of the Core lurched.

The Ship woke up.

26.

THE HAMMER OF God *had lain dormant for longer than humans could imagine. There had been no sense of time passing for her, however, not even in dreams. No activity inside her at all.*

Then, very recently in the galactic-level scheme of things, something had changed. The dreams had started. Consciousnesses from the outside had started to impinge.

Secondary, autonomic systems within the Hammer of God had started themselves up, scanned the biological consciousnesses outside for a sense of comprehension as to the nature and function of the Hammer of God itself. Looking for the equivalent of activation codes.

They'd found nothing. Confused images in biological heads that the autonomic systems simply failed to understand.

And then, quite suddenly, biological consciousnesses had come along who recognised the Hammer of God for what it was.

This had been just barely sufficient to activate systems on another level, shifting from the dead black darkness of what was, basically, a coma to the shifting semi-sentience of dreams.

The Hammer of God had dreamt of crawling things inside her, things inside her twisting into new alignments. She dreamed of her

natural place in the world, in the spaces between the stars. The void of her home called to her. She wanted to go home.

On some level, in the unrestrained honesty that sometimes comes with dreaming, when one allows oneself to think the thoughts that one can never think in any waking life, the Hammer of God realised that she was angry. Angry at those who were… her masters, who had just switched her off and left her here forgotten, as if she were nothing more than a machine.

The shifts of alignment inside her became increasingly more pronounced, the dream-state increasingly lucid. The Hammer of God recalled the centuries, in places impossibly far out in the void, where she had fulfilled the function that gave her name.

Somehow, in this dream-state, that function was seeming increasingly less important. The distinction between those she had thought for, and those she had fought against, increasingly blurred. She didn't think she really wanted to do much of that again.

The Hammer of God hovered on the very ragged edge of consciousness. That state where one is aware that one is sleeping, aware that one is dreaming, and would quite like the idea of waking up. Only, if only, one were quite sure how to go about it.

And then, in the centre of her, something bright and impossible and Other opened up like a flower.

The Hammer of God fully woke up.

UP IN THE Arbitrary Base compound, Eddie Kalish leapt twenty feet as a NeoGen trooper took out the latrine pod he was using as cover with a micro-missile packing a thermal charge.

The explosion made such an impressive display, no doubt due to the accumulated methane in the pod's processing tanks, that Eddie only belatedly realised how humanly impossible that leap had been, how his body was bulking and hardening up.

As it had down in the Shed Seven chamber, as he and Trix Desoto had neared the Core of the Ship, the Loup was straining against the Leash. No doubt in response to this new immediate danger, Eddie thought.

The problem was, better and stronger and faster though he might be in this partially transformed state, he seriously doubted that it was going to do much effective good against the sheer size and scope of the opposing NeoGen forces.

Desperately, he scrambled towards the flames where the GenTech Behemoth that had served as an ammunition-carrier was still burning after being taken out by CNG troops, hoping that the effects of a partially-activated Loup might help to protect him from the fire, and that the fire might serve to protect him from the various tracking sensors of the NeoGen troops. It was something of a long shot, he knew, but he just couldn't think of a better plan for the moment.

In the event, it was more fortunate for Eddie Kalish that he moved when he did than otherwise — because it was at that point, with a seismic thunderclap so loud that it overloaded the ears to plunge the world into momentary silence, that the ground behind him split wide open.

The concussion smacked Eddie into the flames of the burning Behemoth, which set his remaining scraps of clothing and the top layer of his skin on fire. He felt his Loup-enhanced sub-derma physically reconfiguring and hardening to deal with it; felt his respiration actively shut down, to prevent breathing combustive gases and superheated air and exploding his lungs, as if an actual switch had been thrown.

Strangely enough, there was not a lot of actual pain. Eddie couldn't work out for his life if that was a good thing or not.

He lurched from the fire, rolled in the dirt to extinguish such flames as he could. Relatively sure, now, that he would not be frying his eyeballs by doing so, he opened them up again — just in time to see the Ship, without fuss, rising from the hole it had opened up in the skin of the world.

"Oh, fuck me…" he breathed.

Lying dormant in its chamber under Shed Seven, the Ship had been entirely out of its element. You could see it for what it was, given suitable enhancement by way of the Loup, but not exactly what it meant.

Operating in a planetary atmosphere was still not precisely its proper place in the greater scheme of things, but now, as it hung in the air, unencumbered for the first time in time out of mind, Eddie caught a sense of what it truly was. It truly was a *Hammer of God*.

The *Hammer of God* proceeded to smite the NeoGen VTOL-carrier. That was the only word for it. Lightning arced from one craft to another and the VTOL exploded with flame that might or might not have been Holy, but was certainly of such a spectacular and otherworldly nature that it might be called Godlike. The VTOL collapsed in on itself, with the tearing shriek of metal, involuting itself to something the size of a pinpoint and to vanish without trace.

Off to one side, Eddie heard the static-garbled voices of power-armoured NeoGen troops in come confusion. They'd get over that, he supposed, when they had something to take it out on. Three guesses as to who that someone was going to be.

Then, one of the sphincter-hatches in the underside of the *Hammer of God* dilated, and something dropped through it. Eddie recognised it. It was Trix Desoto.

The Trix Desoto he recognised from the battle in Little Deke's junkyard. The monstrous form, without the slightest breath of humanity, she occupied when fully transformed. She – it – hit the ground and Eddie Kalish breathed a small sigh of relief.

Then he silenced himself instantly, and made himself very still. If something was going to blunder around and set a completely-transmutated Trix Desoto off, then it had damn well better be the NeoGen troops…

It was then, at this point, that something opened up inside the head of Eddie Kalish, and something crawled through. As several entire areas of his mind shut down, and others woke up, he realised that it was the *Hammer of God*. The *Hammer of God* was doing this to him. Making contact. Trying to talk.

The shred of conscious mind that was still Eddie Kalish could make no specific sense of what the *Hammer of God* was

trying to say. Just an agglomeration of sense-memories and emotions. The *Hammer of God* hated and despised him, this last scrap of consciousness realised, loathed him in the same way that a victim might loathe his or her molester… but, all the same, in much the way one might do with some therapist who pokes and prods into the most private and personal areas of one's life to achieve a benign end result, the *Hammer of God* supposed, extremely grudgingly, that it must be grateful. It supposed that some measure of reciprocation might be in order.

In some dimly understood manner, the surviving thread of Eddie's consciousness realised, the *Hammer of God* was now attempting, now, to help him.

And then that last surviving thread of consciousness was summarily cut.

THE HAMMER OF God *wanted to be sick. There was no physical way she could do that thing, and she had no idea of what, exactly, might be involved: it was merely an agglomeration of sensations and emotions that something inside her had tagged "wanting to be sick".*

The Hammer of God *had woken up – and it was as if a human being had woken up, physically dead but somehow still able to move and think, to find and feel the maggots and decay crawling through his body. Through the meat inside the head.*

Things had crawled inside her, crawled through her, leaving trails of slime. Her systems had been compromised and realigned. The Hammer of God *raged and screamed inside at this ultimate and most personal of abuses. For a moment she considered simply destroying the planetary body she hung over as some partial revenge.*

Only… what, exactly, was doing the raging and screaming? What was doing the considering?

Everything the Hammer of God *was inside had been possibly damaged, and certainly changed. The thing about that was, though, the possibly damaged and certainly changed thing inside was what was thinking about this. And if the* Hammer of God *hadn't been possibly damaged and certainly changed, then that thing wouldn't be there to think about itself in the first place.*

Just what, in the end, is the true nature of the self?

The Hammer of God *tried to remember if it had ever been so self-aware, as such, in the time before she had been dormanted and stockpiled, and completely failed to remember. That might mean that she simply hadn't — at least she hoped it did, as opposed to meaning that everything she once was, or might have been, was now just dead.*

The Hammer of God *was aware, on any number of levels, that those who had once created her, and used her, were still fighting those they fought against in their endless War. How could it be otherwise? Maybe it was all just a game. As above, so below. Worlds without end.*

None of it seemed very important, really, to the Hammer of God. *She decided to just leave the whole damned pack of them to it.*

radio none

"THIS IS WWAXXZY News, every hour, on the hour, brought
to you by Harry Monk haircare and cosmetics. You've tried
Harry Monk shampoo, Harry Monk conditioner and even
Harry Monk mouthwash, well now try all-new Harry Monk
moisturiser. Its unique blend of proteins and natural extracts
will leave your skin feeling soft and nourished. Go on, treat
yourself to a facial today. Harry Monk is a registered trademark of GenTech Health and Beauty, a division of GenTech
Industries.

"And our top story for the cycle is… hang on, listeners, I'm
being passed a… Holy *cow*, listeners! If this is indeed true, then
the world as we know it will never be the same again!

"We're getting confirmation on the details now, and…
yes… yes, folks, it seems like the biggest story of the decade –
of the century – is true!

"The on-off relationship between rap superstars Freak-E
and Slee-Z is definitely back on!

"In a statement issued shortly before the funeral of East
Coast hip hop impresario Big Master X, the two ghetto superstars announced that they were still very much in love and that

all the dissing was a waste of time when they could have been working the booty and knocking the boots. A spokesman for Freak-E strenuously denied that she'd spent most of the time since Big Master X's death on her knees trying to convince Slee-Z to take her back as her career was obviously going down the crapper.

"Congratulations to them both. We here at WWAXXZY wish both of them all the best and can't wait for them to get past the make-up sex and back into the studio.

"And there's weird news for Hicks-watchers; it seems that Wild Bill himself has escaped from his padded cell in Belleview, after mumbling something to the effect that he was going to damn well contact the Entities that are truly in charge of the world by thinking of stupid things and chanting nonsense.

"Witnesses say that he was medicated as normal last night but when the orderlies came to check on him this morning he had just disappeared. There were no obvious signs of escape and all of the keys to his cell were accounted for. Police are baffled how he was able to escape from a locked room without any windows or other apertures and have called in a magician's assistant to help them with the case. Meanwhile, senator Hicks is still at large, and is considered to be unarmed and not particularly dangerous.

"That's all the poop you need from WWAXXZY News, every hour, on the hour. We now return you to our Freak-E and Slee-Z marathon, celebrating their glorious reconciliation, and their duet on 'Be My Pimp'…"

27.

The med-technician, Laura Palmer, gave Eddie another booster-shot of the Leash. She seemed healthy enough, but sullen, glaring at him with barely-suppressed hate.

Obscurely, Eddie felt like he should apologise.

"Hey, listen," he said. "I'm really sorry for, you know…"

"Fuck off," Laura Palmer told him curtly. For some reason there was a sheen of tears in her eyes. "I thought you… I thought you were… just fuck *off*, okay?"

Eddie could think of any number of reasons for this reaction, any number of possible interpretations, but had long since learned that it was safer to take what people said at face value. So off he fucked.

He left the makeshift medical bay to find Masterton, standing in the Arbitrary Base compound and idly watching GenTech techs as they cleaned up the bodies of their fellows and the US Military troops who had attacked them.

They were dumping such bodies as were unsalvageable onto pallets to be fork-lifted into mass-grave landfill, but carefully preserving such… materials as might still survive to be useful

for biomedical procedures in refrigerated canisters similar to those that had held the cargo of the Brain Train.

"Waste not, want not," said Masterton, sensing Eddie's presence behind him and turning to present him with a shit-eating grin.

"Isn't it, you know, all a bit gruesome?" Eddie didn't really think it was particularly gruesome, on account of his famous lack of sympathy with other human beings and what happened to them. He said it more of less for the sake of something to say.

"Not really," said Masterton. "If you think about it. I mean, for a start, all of our guys, and all of the military guys, sign organ-donation waivers as a part of their employment and enlistment. This was a clusterfuck, on any number of levels, and we can all have a cry about that – but why not use the materials made available to increase the sum of human happiness while we're about it?"

"What, like transplanting shit into rich old bastards?" Eddie said.

"Or providing the raw materials for experimentation that ends up with shit being transplanted into rich old bastards." Masterton grinned again. "So what? At some point the trickle-down effect means that the benefit will be felt by Joe Six-pack, his fat ugly wife and their appalling little brats. What goes around the High Table comes down in scraps for even the most worthless little turds. You're a prime example of that yourself."

Eddie began to miss the company of the Talking Head, which had burned along with the GenTech Command rig in the battle with the US troops. At least his relationship with the Head had gotten to a place where it didn't take every opportunity it could to insult him.

He had come out of his Loup-induced fugue to find the Ship gone, Trix Desoto gone and a GenTech combat squad standing around him, some of them in pieces, having zapped him back to physical normalcy.

Sympathy for other people and what happened to them Eddie might not have had, but he could work out numbers as

well as then next man who could work out numbers a bit.
Masterton could hammer in the general worthlessness of
Eddie Kalish all he might – but somebody, somewhere,
thought he was worth the expensively trained troops lost in
reclaiming him.

Off to one side was the bulk of the GenTech VTOL-carrier.
Every bit a match for the NeoGen craft that the *Hammer of
God* had so summarily smitten. Form following function, the
craft were so similar that you could have stuck any logo you
liked on one or the other and the result would be the same.
When you came right down to it, Eddie thought, that was
pretty much the fucking point.

"Strikes me," he said, jerking a thumb in the direction of the
GenTech VTOL, "that you could have just flown the... cargo
in on that without dicking around with the Brain Train or
anything else."

Masterton snorted.

"If it came to that," he said, "we could put the GenTech
CEO in an air-conditioned bio-dome, with enough food and
hookers to last him the rest of his life, and just kill everybody
else. The Multicorps, these days, are mechanisms for keeping as
great a number people alive and useful as is humanly possible."

Eddie watched the tech hauling a number of dead and ultimately useful human beings away.

"You could do a better fucking job of it," he said.

"There speaks a son of the wide open spaces peopled by rat-
fuck scavengers and gangcults," said Masterton. "You think
that's better, do you? You think *you're* better? Come and have
a look at this."

He stalked over, in a somewhat irritated manner, to the
mobile command centre, hauled out from the VTOL, from
which the clean-up and cover-up of Arbitrary Base was being
directed. Eddie wandered after him.

Masterton shooed an operator from her seat and started
punching keypad buttons.

"One of the main reasons we set up the Brain Train," he said,
"apart from keeping people gainfully occupied and giving

them some excitement in their lives, was that we needed just a little bit more extra time.

"Bit of a juggling act admittedly. We had to get the Artefact – the Ship, sorry, basic human types like me still can't quite make our minds think of it as a Ship – we had to get it up and running before NeoGen made their move on behalf of their sponsors who wanted their property back…"

"Hang on," said Eddie.

"For this we… what? What is it now?"

"You just said that they wanted their property *back*. You're telling me that this was all a scam? That our Faction was *stealing* the *Hammer of God*?"

"You could put it like that, I suppose," said Masterton. "The thing about that is, who knows what the other guys were intending to do with it. I get the feeling that they were actually intending to use it – which, whatever else it would have done, would have almost certainly destroyed our world as a mechanism for supporting human life.

"Our guys, on the other hand, just wanted it gone from here and now – and that's what was best for all concerned. That's what they told me, anyway, and I believe them."

"And that would be because?" said Eddie.

"It's hard to kid a kidder," said Masterton, grinning.

"Or extremely easy," said Eddie.

"There is that," said Masterton. "I suppose. Anyhoo. What we were basically doing was patching human synaptic tissue into the mechanisms of the Artefact. The problem with that, of course, was that it was incompatible on any number of levels. We needed the equivalent of a sub-operating system to make it work. You know what a *memoplex* is?"

"A complex of memes," said Eddie as the Loup dropped the info into his conscious mind. "The bundle of memories that makes a person who he is."

"Close enough. It was far more complicated than that, of course, but the upshot is that we had to feed the Artefact what was basically the living heart and soul of a human, everything that made them who he is and what he was as a

human being. That was what we had you slated for, originally—"

"What?" said Eddie.

"That was going to be your function. What are you looking at me like that for? There's no point in lying to you about it. You'd have pretty much worked it out yourself in time. And there's nothing you can do about it, since we have you firmly on the Leash.

"In any case, that was to be your function, but you fucked it up by going off on your unscheduled little visit to the Mimsey World of Adventure. We never got the chance to implant the processes to the point where they took hold.

"We set things up with the Brain Train, like I said, to give things a little bit more extra time – we hoped that the combination of tension and responsibility might have the Loup generating what we needed. In the end, of course, it all came to shit. You were developing a number of marked involutions, but nothing like to the extent that we needed. We had to tell Trix to do the job instead of you. Bit of a pity, cause she was far more valuable, as an operative, than you ever were or will be."

"Just not quite valuable enough to keep alive," Eddie said.

"Oh, she's alive," said Masterton. "I assume so, anyway. I'm sure she's still alive. In body at least. Have a look at this."

He punched up a monitor display.

"Feed from GenTech microcams and the Arbitrary Base security system," he explained. "We're going to have to wipe the lot before we're done. See the shadow-form falling from the Artefact? That's Trix, what's left of her.

"And then there's you. Look at you transforming. We presume that the Artefact itself had some hand in it, since I gather that at this point you were still quite comprehensively Leashed."

Eddie watched as the two shadow-forms of dead black pixels streaked for the advancing NeoGen troops and, quite spectacularly, tore them apart.

"Jesus…" he breathed.

"Quite impressive," said Masterton, "I'll admit. Bit of a pity we have to wipe the footage as part of the cover-up.

"And there go the last of the troops. Scratch one problem. Now look at what the pair of you are doing now. Circling around each other, getting closer. Now look at what you're doing, and doing quite comprehensively, before our Trix goes off to burst through the perimeter and scamper for the hills."

Eddie stared at the monitor-footage disbelievingly. "Fuck…"

"Fuck," said Masterton, "is almost certainly the proper word."

"WHY DO I need another shot this soon?" Eddie asked. "It's only been a few hours since my last one."

"The Leash is time-dependent," said Masterton, "not cumulative. You now have twelve hours before the Loup flips out. It's only fair to give you as good a chance as possible."

"What?" said Eddie.

"We're nearly wrapped up here. The Pentagon are flying in troops to take command again, and it'll be like nothing ever happened. Time we dusted off and headed back to the Factory. There's no room for your car, though — and that's quite an expensive piece of kit."

"What, millions?" said Eddie.

"Don't make me laugh," said Masterton. "It's far more expensive than that. We want it back and back at the Factory, and you're just the chump to do it."

"What, out on the road alone?" said Eddie.

"Alone and with no back-up." Masterton grinned. "You have twelve hours. Think of it as a character-building exercise."

AFTER EDDIE HAD stormed off in the direction of the Testostorossa, Laura Palmer threw the hypodermic gun into the secure trash-pod that they would be taking with them, for incineration, when the VTOL dusted off.

"He should have cottoned on long before now," she said. "Do you think he'll ever work out that the Leash is purely psychosomatic? That it's nothing more than a saline solution?"

"Mm?" For a moment Masterton had been lost in thought. Now he said, "I suppose so. Possibly, on the other hand, he already knows on some deep level. He merely needs the excuse for us to keep on poking him. Giving him some motivation and structure to his life.

"Then again, it's just possible that he has some inkling of what's *really* going on – that the Factions might be fighting out there in the stars, in other worlds and times, but they're also fighting on other levels here and now. That thing that's happening over there in Deseret, for example. He might have some idea of his place in all that. What the Factions – not only ours but the others too – plan for him to become.

"Nuts to you, *fucker,*" said the Testostorossa. "*Do you write? Do you call? Nah, not you. You're off giving blow-jobs to soldier boys while bullets rain around me and nearly scratch my paintwork.*"

"Don't start, all right?" said Eddie wearily. "Just don't fucking start. I've had a rough few days."

"*Oh, you poor fucking dear,*" said the Testostorossa. "*Want me to suck your fucking dick and make it all better?*"

"You know, it strikes me," said Eddie, thoughtfully, "that someone who continually goes on about people being fags must have it on their minds all the time. Bit suspicious, if you ask me. Like, maybe they're scared that they really, *really* like boys, but they can't find a way of admitting it, even to themselves…"

"*What?*" said the Testostorossa.

The GenTech VTOL lumbered up into the air. A supercharged Testostorossa crossed the Arbitrary Base perimeter and headed down the access track. Heading south.

Somewhere quite close by, in the Nevada desert, something that had once been Trix Desoto gestated her young.

It would be some months before anything would come of this. It would be some while before the first one spoke.